STRAMFORD'S ABBEY

Woodbridge Publishers

1200 Century Way, Thorpe Park,
Leeds, LS158ZA

First Edition

ISBN (Paperback): 978-1-917184-14-4

ISBN (Hardback): 978-1-917184-15-1

Cover Design by Woodbridge Publishers

WOODBRIDGE
PUBLISHERS

Dedication

For my inspirational husband and children, they are truly great people.

Thank you, Dad, for formatting and editing, especially with regard to speech marks!

Big thanks to Woodbridge Publishers for your support with my first book!

Table of Contents

Chapter 1

All was peaceful about the grounds of the Abbey. Autumn had arrived, and trees dropped curling orange leaves carelessly about the grass. What leaves remained whispered conspiratorially in the breeze. Had they spoken, they would recount yesterday's bloody assassination witnessed right under their shady boughs. They'd remember the pulsed spurts of warm blood upon their trunks, the shrieks of terror dwarfed by the huge skyscape above their crowns. The victim curling round and around, churning the grass into a soup of mud, blood and saliva. A white face turned into the earth and bit hard into the grass in a final desperate plea to live.

By the following morning, all that could be seen was a mere abrasion under the largest tree. The night's rain had moved the bloody soup into gentle rivulets that fed the thirsty tree roots. The silent oaks stood uniformly in a line, unfazed, timeless.

On a drizzly October morning, a young woman boarded a train. She wore expensive clothes, knee-high boots and oversized sunglasses. With well-rehearsed composure, she walked down the carriage. Eyes peered curiously over phones, a chewing girl, a bespectacled businessman, pensioners, tourists. She was not tall, though she held herself to her full height; her expression was haughty, though whether that was from a genuine superiority complex or a mask to hide deep insecurities, it was impossible to tell.

"Oi!" shouted a youth.

Turning in surprise, the woman saw a red-faced boy of around 12 tenderly rubbing his ear and, with the other hand, inadvertently lassoing her with the wire from his earphones.

"Sorry?" she lowered her sunglasses to look over them.

"If you've broke 'em..." he mumbled, his gaze taking her in.

Pulling the rucksack from her back, she saw that, somehow, she'd managed to hook one of the child's earphones onto the gold clasp and, with quite a force, popped the other from his ear.

"Have I damaged them?" she raised an eyebrow, scanning for witnesses.

A few newspapers rustled, and the gum-chewing girl stared.

"Naw..." he turned back to his seat, embarrassed.

Passing through two more carriages, she noticed a sharp decline in seat availability and with the train nearing a stop, she settled for a forward-facing table seat.

Opening the clasp on her rucksack, she did a quick scan of the contents. "Essentials only Charlotte!" her father had advised. "All else will be provided at the Abbey Sanctuary."

Charlotte mused at the words. 'Sanctuary'. A place of refuge... rather a strange name for a luxury Spa. Her father had implored her to be open-minded, to allow healing to take place.

The train slowed to a standstill; moving boards shouted about smooth milk chocolate and cheap car insurance. Several people walked quickly towards the train, while others squinted at the flickering arrivals screens.

"The next train to arrive at platform 2 is the... 13:18 Central Train service to London Paddington calling at..."

Charlotte turned away from the window to look at the people stepping through the carriages, some flustered, others calm and mechanical.

A middle-aged man with a pronounced belly and most commendable moustache stepped aboard, pausing at the empty seat. He glanced inquisitively at Charlotte, and she nodded with the faintest of smiles. He sat heavily opposite her and withdrew a mobile from his top pocket. Charlotte turned her head to one side and gazed out of the window; the train moved off again. The station broke into a roofscape, then industrial buildings, and eventually, open fields. Charlotte could see her reflection in the glass. She did not much care for the changing scenery.

Some time passed, and the stations became further apart. Checking her phone and setting herself a reminder alarm, she allowed herself to doze off.

"You have lost your way. You should be okay, but you need help. Without guidance, you will become a danger to yourself and others."

Suddenly, with a jolt, Charlotte kicked out. The moustached gentleman grimaced and quickly bent to rub his shin.

"Oh, oh, I'm sorry!" Charlotte muttered, realising her accidental assault.

"You were probably dreaming," he spoke whilst rubbing his shin.

When he lifted his head, the corners of his moustache rose slightly as if a smile was hidden deep in the undergrowth.

"The train is now approaching Ecklesford Street Station, where this service will be terminating. All change please, all change..."

Waiting for the train to stop entirely, Charlotte tied her scarf around her neck and pulled her rucksack to her back. She joined the bustle of people by the door and stepped off.

The roads became quieter as the driver guided his cab out of the city. Large houses with expensively paved driveways boasted four-by-fours and expensive security lighting. The gardens were manicured, and the gates loomed large. Soon though, houses got smaller and more tightly packed, wheelie

4

bins littered the pavements and old chip shop newspapers threw their stories around the gutters...

"Are you sure this is the right place?" Charlotte spoke at last, snapping shut her phone.

"uh hu"

"But why would a Spa and Spiritual retreat be in a place like this?"

The cab driver sniffed and scratched behind his ear.

"Dunno love... it's an old Abbey, ain't it? But wasn't it a school a long time ago? me mam said it was... pretty fuckin weird, still... maybe it's nice now... an Abbey full uh nuns huh? You a nun or summat?"

With this, he exploded into an unpleasant sort of laugh, and Charlotte looked out of the window.

"Here," he said at last, swerving the car around to the right.

With a skid on the loose gravel, he stopped by some imposing wrought iron gates. They were flanked by very high stone walls with razor wire just visible at the top. Nothing of the spiritual radiated from that entrance, but rather, 'military jail,' thought Charlotte. Releasing her seat belt and stepping out of the taxi, she supposed that it must have been a rather exclusive retreat, therefore, security would have to be very tight.

5

"Right, love, that'll be sixty-eight pounds."

She produced three twenties and a ten and waited for the change.

The car sped off and left Charlotte alone with the huge gates. They were locked.

Reaching into her pocket for her mobile, Charlotte suddenly felt apprehensive. Just when she started to consider calling for another taxi home, she noticed a girl of no more than 20 behind the gates. She was dressed from head to foot in a traditional nun's habit.

"Can I help you?" she inquired from behind the bars.

"Oh, I'm expected, by…. er… Mother Pascal, I think. My father… made inquiries…"

She tried not to stare, but the stranger looked straight out of a film set.

"What is your name please?"

"Charlotte… Charlotte Compton"

With a warm smile, the sister stepped back from the gates and moved out of sight. With an impressive grinding sound, the huge gates began to open, revealing behind them a wide cobbled path lined with oak trees. Behind these, the land seemed to stretch into fields on one side and woodland on the other. It was certainly very beautiful, even through the dulling autumn sky.

"I am Sister Bernadine. Take my hand," she smiled again.

"Er... your hand?!..." Charlotte unsuccessfully held back an embarrassed giggle, "I'm okay... thanks."

"May I take your bag? It is quite a journey to the cloister."

"No, I'm fine carrying it."

She put her sunglasses up on her head and released tendrils of hair from behind her ears. Pulling her ponytail through her fingers, she finally relaxed. She had arrived.

"Have you travelled far?"

"Not too far."

The gates clanked shut, and large mechanical bolts slid across. The two walked in silence for several minutes, Charlotte enjoying the old cobbles.

"Some people find it easier to walk on this verge. The cobbles are rather aggressive underfoot, especially if your soles are thin."

"Oh, I quite like them," Charlotte smiled, showing perfect teeth, "They kinda remind me of a supermarket near our house when I was little. There was a little patch of cobbles and all the kids in the town used to walk over them while their mums got a trolley."

The young nun nodded and, in her singsong voice, said, "Children are so innocent, aren't they? They will accept that Noah built an ark or that Moses spoke to the burning bush. They are not suspicious at all about the truth of these stories."

Seemingly a rather bizarre take on her supermarket trolly story, Charlotte supposed nuns always mentioned something religious in much of what they said, so she replied slightly sarcastically.

"Yes, but that's just because kids don't know any better; they also believe in Santa."

"Indeed, but it does not matter what they believe. What is important is that they do believe. They have the capacity for accepting God into their hearts."

Charlotte bit her tongue and, remembering her father's cautionary words, chose to say nothing.

"Welcome to Stramford's Abbey!" announced Sister Bernadine, nodding towards the great stone building with a magnificent spire.

Chapter 2

Approaching the beautiful old building, Charlotte was surprised and rather disappointed to be guided off the main path and around the side to a row of small brick structures like offices or small houses. Behind those was a series of portacabins with net curtains masking the windows. They looked dingy and sad in sharp contrast to the magnificence of the Abbey.

"Is this where the staff sleep?" Charlotte asked, taking her sunglasses from the top of her head and replacing them on her face. She lifted them up and looked again as if the tint might reduce the grimness.

"They are indeed sleeping quarters," Bernadine replied, watching Charlotte closely.

"That's not where I'll be staying, right?" Charlotte smiled at her companion.

"I'm afraid I don't know your sleeping arrangements at present," she replied a little coolly.

They continued past the dwellings, and a large modern building came into view. There were ventilation hoods and a large industrial-sized launderette evident, as well as half-open windows of what appeared to be a big kitchen. It was not what Charlotte had expected at all. A group of denim-clad men in high-vis jackets stood smoking and chatting quietly at the entrance...

"With er... with all due respect," began Charlotte as the two women entered the building, "er... I would have expected something a little more... I don't know... more refined perhaps?"

"Refined?"

"Yeah, like, like a swimming pool maybe? Or health treatment rooms? There's massage therapy, right?"

Bernadine smiled and stopped by some double doors.

"There is indeed a swimming pool," she said, her eyes looking away from Charlotte to a collection of paintings that hung on the walls.

"Do you like them?" she asked.

The paintings were large and colourful, evidently themed on Bible stories. Charlotte looked from one to the other and, on close inspection, realised that they were actually quite gory...

The first painting was done in a series of blues and pinks. In a thick black outline, someone had painted a Jesus figure on the cross with his eyes looking at the heavens. Around the thorny crown, great dobs of red paint covered Jesus' head and neck. His flesh was a poster pink, which clashed jarringly with the scarlet blood. The remaining paintings had a similar child-like application, with fingerprints dotted around the works. The last painting, which depicted a dove with an olive branch in its beak, showed numerous paint drips that had run down and hardened, giving the painting a depressing feel.

"These are... done by children?" Charlotte eventually asked.

"No, the Praise group worked together to create this one here," she said, pointing to the most repulsive one of all.

"This one was a donation by a former sister."

"The Praise group?"

"Yes. They are a group who, with assistance, partake in various activities such as painting, crafts, cookery and sports. These are often themed on the greatness of God. More often than not, this group will use these opportunities to give thanks to the Abbey and to our Lord and Saviour."

Charlotte grimaced in embarrassment.

"I didn't know this... experience was going to be so... religious," she said the word with unhidden contempt.

"I thought it was going to be a bit spiritual or something, but..."

Bernadine looked directly at her with a pleasant expression.

"I know it can be a little overwhelming."

"Er... so, the Praise group, they aren't kids, are they? I thought it was adults only here."

"No, although many have the innocence of children. Some of them have rather complex needs. You will see that when we pass through their recreation room now."

They left the paintings to walk through the double doors. A corridor followed with a distinct stench of gym shoes. A corkboard of leaflets flapped as they passed, Charlotte managing to catch sight of just a few headings: 'Pottery class, choir practice, recreation, prayer, weekday groups.' They passed several shut doors. A few drawings hung crookedly on notice boards. One door had a rather impressive gold plaque with "Sir E Stramford" carved into the bronze.

Suddenly, Sister Bernadine slowed and looked directly at Charlotte.

With palpable apprehension, she whispered, "I feel I should warn... no, no I..."

She blushed and looked away.

"God forgive me, but the appearance of these people is somewhat... distressing..."

She winced as if saying these words was so sinful it created physical pain.

"The Praise group?" Charlotte offered.

"Yes, they have sadly been rejected from society, but they... they have souls of... purest," she tailed off and opened the door.

A strange gurgling and hissing stung Charlotte's ears as she stepped into the room. Though the room itself was cheerily decorated, she saw the sounds came from a grey-haired man writhing around in a chair. His eyes bulged, goggling almost out of their sockets. Charlotte tore her gaze away and scanned the room. She counted numerous poor souls who were masked by tumours or burns, some grotesquely deformed.

One blonde lady looked as if she had been in a terrible fire, as her face missed a nose entirely, and one eye was sealed shut. In sharp contrast, the skin on the other side of her face looked smooth and youthful. A bearded man wore a cloth bib; he was suffering from a large tumour that obstructed much of his mouth. He gargled deep, unsettling sounds, yet in his hand, he held a small chisel and seemed to be constructing a very intricate wooden ship. The sails were missing, yet every other detail was there in perfect miniature form. A Down syndrome man stood washing up at the sink, handing the wet plates to his worker, who dried them and popped them away neatly.

Within minutes, as the initial horror began to ebb away, Charlotte saw staff in red polo shirts dotted about the room.

13

Many nodded or gave her a small wave as she unashamedly stared at the praise group's scars, tumours and burns that transformed their faces so cruelly.

Over by the window, an older member of staff sat opposite a wizened-looking figure deeply absorbed in a game of chess. To the left of the pair sat a circle of five visually impaired people on plastic chairs. Charlotte watched the rather sharp-looking lady in the distinctive red polo shirt; she had a tablet device that seemed to connect to the headphones of all participants. She scribbled notes as they listened while opening another tablet device and scrolling through quickly.

"They are studying Baroque music at the moment," Bernadine whispered to Charlotte, "A lot of Bach, Puccini, and Handel are moving on to Purcell as we reach the end of the month. It's a really fascinating course and lends itself so well to our regular choir rehearsals."

A strange moaning sound caused Charlotte to whisk around, only to see a small mixed-race boy dabbing a paintbrush on an enlarged outline of a rainbow. He looked painfully thin, and his face squinted in concentration as he painted. Each time he put the brush upon the paper he would begin a low moan, which would crescendo until the brush lifted.

"This painting shows God's rainbow over Noah's Ark," explained Bernadine, watching Charlotte closely.

"He's only a boy," Charlotte managed to whisper.

"No, Michael is actually in his early twenties, but he has an undiagnosed degenerate disease that stops him from growing to adult size and causes progressively severe learning difficulties as he ages."

Charlotte could not explain what stopped her from marching straight out of the building to catch the first available taxi and demand to be taken home. Perhaps it was guilt, shock, or even a morbid curiosity.

After a short time, Bernadine guided Charlotte out of the room and back into the corridor.

"Who are those people?" Charlotte whispered

"They are souls who cannot exist in society. They're banished from your world. They will live out their lives here without judgement or prejudice."

"But where did they come from, and who pays for them?"

"We receive... funding."

"From who?"

Sister Bernadine did not answer as she closed the door gently behind them.

"Why did you show them to me?" asked Charlotte numbly, "I mean, it's sad and all that, but what does it have to do with me?"

Bernadine smiled kindly and said, "We are now going to see Mother Pascal."

A grand-looking set of double doors revealed the beautiful interior of a large priory. There were pews on either side, and a great organ dominated the left wall. Imposing stained glass windows depicted the Pentecost; to the right, the vast window shone with the Adoration of the Magi.

"The old Crypt is still here, and the monks' cells are still attached to the church; however, the modern extensions were due to the school that ran here up until 10 years ago," Bernadine said as they walked together.

"Why is it not a school anymore?" asked Charlotte, glancing at the tomb of a long-gone king.

"There was a tragedy which forced the school to close. Even when it opened its doors again, people were too superstitious and fearful to send their children here, so it lay destitute for years. It was only when the nuns of Bermondsey Abbey relocated to this Abbey that it became inhabited again."

"What sort of tragedy?"

"A child committed suicide, but rather than it being a one-off tragic accident, it seemed to spur on other children to do the same. There was a mass suicide attempt by six children. It was extremely distressing, and even though an inquiry took place, nothing came to light. The bishop of

London travelled to the Abbey and blessed it. The nuns took this benediction with sincere gratitude and vowed to turn the unhappy memories of this place into hope and praise for God."

"Right, so it is a nunnery then, like the cabbie said. Not a spa break, which is what I was told," Charlotte pursed her lips in frustration.

"Can I be so bold as to suggest it is neither?" Bernadine said gently, "Once the nuns were established, Mr Edward Stramford purchased the Abbey and all the surrounding land and created Stramford's Abbey, a Sanctuary of healing following a Christian ethos, that of compassion and love. It is a place where all its inhabitants are given the opportunity to thrive and reach their potential without judgement or societal constraints."

"Right, okay then…" Charlotte muttered sarcastically, but in a louder voice, she said, "So there are spa facilities here then?"

"There is everything that you need to reach your optimum health and happiness," Bernadine smiled.

Charlotte felt an increasing dislike for her companion; sweet though she was, it seemed she was reciting a pre-scripted sales pitch. There was no waver in her delivery; perhaps she was an example of Christian perfection.

Stretching out her hand, Charlotte traced the ornate carvings of the wooden pews. They were in very good condition and beautifully polished, intricately hand-stitched prayer cushions were aligned with hymn books and placed in neat rows. Reaching over to take a hymn book, she noticed Sister Bernadine walking without a sound towards the altar; Charlotte frowned. She felt like an alien as she studied her guide, an ethereal creature not quite of this world.

Turning away, she began thumbing through the pages of the old book. Smiling privately, she recognised hymns she knew so well, 'Hah! 'All things bright and beautiful, God is love, Glad that I live am I.' Humming quietly, she sat in the pew nearest and continued to flick through the hymn book 'Rejoice! The Lord is King, Stand up, Stand up for Jesus'.

A tap on the shoulder brought her out of her trance and caused her to guiltily place the hymn book back down in its original place.

"Do not be afraid. You are most welcome to praise God through these hymns. We do have a very popular church choir."

Charlotte grew uncomfortable at the closeness of the person.

"I see by enjoying these hymns of praise, you have set aside a place in your heart for God," the stranger continued, her low voice quiet though assertive…

"No… no hold it, just… just hang on a moment there."

Charlotte looked up at the woman. From her seated position, the perspective was all wrong, and the woman looked unnaturally tall.

"I'm just… looking, looking through a few hymns I knew as a kid… I'm not setting aside places in my heart… or joining any choir for that matter, especially a church one!" trailing off, she rose to her feet.

Her knees seemed awkwardly big against the tight pew. The lady who had spoken did not move out of the way.

"I'm here solely on the wishes of my dad… as a spiritual retreat type of place, healing stuff, like a Spa break, you know?"

She looked up at the face of the stranger who had blocked her into the pew. The two women stared at each other in silence. The taller appeared to be stifling dislike with a strangely forced smile.

Finally, unable to bear the charged atmosphere any longer, Charlotte blurted out, "Excuse me!" and all but shoved her way out of the pew.

The nun sidestepped slightly to allow her through, yet her habit brushed intrusively upon her.

"Mother Pascal," smiled the tall figure offering a hand.

"Charlotte Compton."

"Yes, I know who you are," she said, "Please come with me. Do you have a bag or belongings with you?"

"Oh!" Charlotte called in dismay, "I must have left my rucksack in the entrance hall when I was looking at the paintings."

"Don't worry, I'll retrace our steps and find it!" came the voice of Sister Bernadine as she came to join them.

"Thank you, Sister," nodded Mother Pascal.

Then, turning to Charlotte, she said, "Your bag will be quite safe in this building."

Charlotte studied Mother Pascal. She was tall for a woman, perhaps 6 ft, mid-fifties, with an intense and rather masculine face. It was the sort of face Charlotte thought one would struggle to warm to.

On exiting the church, the two walked briskly in a draughty corridor. Outside, Charlotte could see cave-like structures that looked weather-beaten and ancient.

"Are these the old Monks' cells the other lady... Bernadine, was on about?" asked Charlotte brightly in an effort to lighten the rather awkward atmosphere.

"They are."

"Are they used for anything now?"

20

"Sometimes in the summer, the sisters use them for quiet meditation and prayer. However, they are seldom used in the winter months."

The end of the cells opened out into the churchyard, and Charlotte looked with interest at the vast array of headstones, tombs and statues ordered on the most green and mossy grass. They looked predominantly Victorian, with great stone tributes placed to once noble families; she read them as they passed Culpepper, Stevenson, and Hastings. Many of the inscriptions had faded, eroded by decades of harsh weather. Mosses and lichens grew happily on fallen headstones and managed to creep up to the rather beautiful stone faces of cherubs and angels.

The two women walked in silence across the cemetery. Charlotte was enjoying the bouncy moss underfoot, and she longed to reach down and touch it with her fingers to see if it felt warm. The peace was disturbed by crows cawing and flapping overhead, and Charlotte couldn't help but notice that the flapping mirrored Mother Pascal's black habit.

At the end of the cemetery, they turned back towards the portacabins Charlotte had seen earlier. They were painted a deep grey, which answered the evening sky perfectly.

"This is where you will be sleeping" said Pascal, motioning Charlotte to climb the three steps first.

Not sure whether to begin her protests then or allow her curiosity to be tempted further, Charlotte took a step...

Within the cabin, she saw four simple beds a few metres apart, with a small chest of drawers and a circular rug for each. There was no linen on the bed, only blankets underneath.

"Hang on… I'm sorry, but what the actual hell is this?" Charlotte gestured to the beds incredulously.

"I am not staying in a cabin like this, no offence, but it's like a donkey shed!"

She took her sunglasses from the top of her head and used them to identify examples of the appalling conditions. An awkward silence thickened the air. So Charlotte filled it.

"I'm especially not sharing with complete strangers. I'm sorry if you were expecting someone different or something, but there's definitely been a mistake!"

With a tone that did not attempt to mask her contempt, Mother Pascal eventually replied, "You have an hour before the refectory opens for supper and prayers."

Then, turning on her heel, she left Charlotte alone in the cabin.

The conflict depressed her, but after some reflection, she decided to accept the room for the night, but she ensured things changed by the morning. Reaching over to one of the lamps, she flicked it on. An orangey glow fell onto the Bible resting on the side table. The silver cross on the front cover reflected the light, causing it to glow unnaturally bright.

Swearing under her breath, she picked up the book and crammed it into the drawer before flopping on the nearest bed with her phone.

Almost immediately, there was a knock on the door.

"Charlotte? I have your bag," called Bernadine.

"Sure, yeah. Put it over there!" she muttered, not looking up from her phone.

"How come there's no bloody signal here? How am I supposed to make calls?"

Charlotte looked up in frustration, expecting to see the young nun in the same attire as before.

"You've changed," she said, surprised at the casual red polo shirt and jeans.

"Yes, we wear the traditional habit for special occasions as well as prayer and worship. The choir is expected to wear it, too."

"It's kind of nice to see you looking so normal," blurted Charlotte.

"Did I look abnormal before?" replied Sister Bernadine with a smile.

"I'm sure you've found the bathroom already. There are towels and flannels there. The Bible is yours, too. There are additional blankets under the bed, and there are bathroom cabinets in the next room for your toiletries."

"Er... look, I'm sorry to sound ungrateful or anything, but this is literally... a shed. I understand my father must have paid for this... experience. I'm not sure he would be too pleased about this."

Bernadine smiled politely.

"I understand it may be a little different to what you're used to, but I can assure you, the room will be most comfortable."

"Well, I'll accept it tonight, but by tomorrow, I'm going to put in a complaint and get moved," Charlotte asserted.

Taking her bag from Bernadine, she began pulling the contents onto the bed.

"What time is dinner?" she called, rummaging through her clothes, "Are we going smart casual? Or is it more formal?"

She took out a multipack of earrings from her bag pocket and laid them out. Perhaps the dining hall would be a little salubrious, meriting a more glamorous look. She rummaged in the bottom of her bag for her perfume. She had wrapped it up in her sleeping mask for protection. Giving herself a quick spritz to freshen up, she felt better. It was to be expected that there would be minor issues to address when trying something new. Once she had booked in for her first massage and facial, things would most likely fall into place. She could just refuse all the spiritual workshops and wouldn't need to see that horse-faced Mother Pascal woman at all.

Her phone buzzed and she picked it up; still the internet did not appear to be working. She would need to ask Bernadine for the Wi-Fi password. Perhaps she could just ring her dad using an old-fashioned phone call. No. There was no signal. She looked up as the door closed with a thud.

Chapter 3

Charlotte began to wander around the cabin, taking photos of the substandard living conditions she was going to have to put up with for the night. These photos would be given as evidence to her father or whoever was responsible for the sleeping arrangements. It was quite possible her dad had been duped into paying for something his daughter had not had the pleasure of receiving, but the truth would come out and at the very least, she should be offered some sort of compensation, perhaps an extra voucher for one of the beauty treatments or the therapy sessions. Sitting on the bed, she scrolled through the photos.

Suddenly, with quite a bang, the door flew open.

A small but broad-shouldered woman, heavily wrinkled with short grey hair, kicked her rucksack into the room and followed it in, brows knitted in suspicion as she surveyed the room. Oddly enough, she seemed not to notice Charlotte for several moments.

"Hello?"

"Whassat?" the lady spun round most youthfully, then noticed Charlotte at last.

"Hello m'love, they got you roped up here n'all have they?"

"Er… yeah, you could say that. I'm Charlotte… I literally just arrived."

"Oh 'ave yu?" she walked over to an empty bed and threw her backpack down. Turning to Charlotte, she smiled, showing neat dentures.

"Patricia… Pat to you," she paused to light a cigarette, studying Charlotte with wrinkled eyes.

"Are we?… are we allowed to smoke?"

"Oh no, love, no we ain't," she winked and took a deep drag.

She offered the packet to Charlotte and when she politely refused, set about opening the cabin windows.

"We have to get ready for dinner, right? That Pascal woman, who I don't think likes me that much, was saying something about a refectory?"

Pat stopped what she was doing and studied Charlotte for a moment.

"You've fallen out with 'er already 'ave yu?"

She smiled mischievously before taking a long drag on her cigarette.

"Don't worry love, I fell out with everybody at your age. 'aving said all that, I'd tone it down if I were you, that 'Pascal woman' as you call 'er… is the most uptight wuman I ever saw, an' if there's one thing she cannot stand... it's insubordination."

"Yeah, well, we'll see," muttered Charlotte as she took her toiletries bag to the bathroom and began applying a top-up of powder and lip colour.

Finally, she left the bathroom with a spruce of perfume and rejoined Pat.

"Really darlin' there ain't no need to be dressin' up. You do look nice though."

Unable to answer because of a sharp knock on the door, both women were distracted by the tall figure of Mother Pascal peering into the cabin.

"I sincerely hope that you have not been smoking in here."

"Oh no, Mother Pascal, you are very much mistaken, filthy habit if you ask me," retorted Pat in her gravelliest voice.

The look of distaste on Mother Pascal's face was so pronounced that Charlotte had to stifle a laugh.

"Come this way and I will direct you to the refectory," she smiled unconvincingly.

The three women walked briskly across the grounds, arriving at the refectory within minutes. Large folding tables joined to make 3 rows. Two were already filled with nuns in traditional habits. On the remaining table sat an array of red-shirted women and an occasional non-uniformed person looking a little out of place. Charlotte and her new companion followed the other tables, where others were eating their simple meal in silence. There were prayers and occasional scrapes of cutlery against crockery. The tables appeared to get dismissed one by one, although Charlotte could not see who was directing them. Once the plates were taken away, Charlotte's table filed out almost militarily. Back at the cabin, Charlotte was wholly unnerved to find that her bag along with all her possessions, had disappeared. No phone, no clothes, nothing.

"Where the hell is my stuff?!" Charlotte repeated over and over until Pat finally broke in.

"It's been taken for Christ's sake! They've taken away your stuff, all the temptations of your wicked heathen ways, no doubt."

Pat shook her head in disgust, "They'll be takin' away your whole identity soon, just you wait!"

Charlotte looked closely at her roommate; she was probably right. She should have expected something extreme like this, a complete detox of modern life... or something.

Unwillingly resigned to her situation, she sighed and looked at the plain white nightdress, a red polo shirt and elasticated jeans that were folded on all the beds. After some investigation, the bathroom revealed toothpaste, four toothbrushes, towels, and a large bottle of presumably shampoo or soap. On reflection, Charlotte decided that she didn't care so much about her clothes and toiletries, but she had so wanted to text her dad to say she'd arrived safely but also to tell him what an appalling dump the Abbey had turned out to be.

Pat was seething about her cigarettes as her night-time fag was the most important one of all, she said. Barely another word was shared between the new roommates as they climbed into bed and pulled up the rough woollen blankets.

It couldn't have been much after midnight when the cabin door clicked open. There were muffled whispers and shuffling feet. Charlotte sat bolt upright but immediately felt a palm clap across her mouth. Her arms were seized, and without knowing how, she was bundled out of the room in nothing but her nightdress. She looked from one figure to the other but could see no detail, only shadows. The profile of a man spat a whisper, which resulted in some sort of cloth being pulled across Charlotte's eyes.

The small group walked for a considerable amount of time, turning corners and opening and shutting doors. Once, Charlotte tripped on some stairs and was saved by such a cruel grip upon her shoulder that she cried out.

Then they stopped. And just as instantly as they had appeared, they disappeared. Loosening their vice-like grips, they let go, leaving Charlotte shaking with her hands raised protectively to her face.

Very slowly and cautiously, she removed the cloth from her eyes and, through the gloomy lighting, saw four figures seated behind a long table. The room was a simple square with grey walls and a wine carpet, yet on every wall space hung huge Caravaggio-style paintings, some of which Charlotte recognised, others she did not. The chiaroscuro gave the paintings an intensity that was reflected almost exactly in the expressions at the table.

"What the hell is this?"

"Charlotte, you are at the first step of your redemption."

"Redemption?!" She scoffed, "I hardly think being… being… blindfolded… and… and bloody manhandled…" she tailed off.

"This is not a Spa break, my dear," came the voice of the tall man.

Charlotte pulled at her nightdress, cold and vulnerable.

"What the hell am I doing here? Who are you? I'm sorry, but there's been one hell of a mix-up. This is definitely not what my father requested."

"Please take the chair behind you. Before you can make the first steps to recovery, you will need to accept full responsibility for your actions, past and present," the man continued.

"You have been brought here to save you from a path of self-destruction."

"Self-destruction? What the bloody hell kind of nonsense are you talking about?"

A mighty bang came from Mother Pascal, who slammed her hand upon the table.

"A little respect!" she hissed, "You are to stand before God and seek his forgiveness. You have sinned; that is why you are here. You have sinned (God help you), and only by clutching at the feet of Christ the Lord and begging his forgiveness... can you be saved."

"What!? What... is this... Oh, come on. Point out my frailties by all means, but you can't... attempt to indoctrinate me like this... it's ludicrous... it's stupid!"

Charlotte looked from one face to another. Fear crept in from somewhere in her throat.

"I'm not making peace with your god," she said quietly, looking directly at Pascal.

She allowed her gaze to drift to the tall man, who looked as if he was trying to solve a conundrum. The bearded man next to him seemed to drill his eyes right inside her. How could she possibly plead her case to any of these people?

"Spiritual enlightenment is generic, surely? That's why I'm here, right? I don't have to subscribe to your Christian faith to... to heal, do I?" Charlotte felt bolder as she explained, "I get it... I get that I have to be sorry for all the stuff I've done, and I am."

She backed away from the single chair.

"But I won't apologise to you!"

Suddenly, she felt a hand upon her shoulder. It tightened, causing her to wince. It belonged to the red-haired staff member Charlotte instantly recognised from the Praise group. Mother Pascal continued as Charlotte was physically directed to the chair.

"You have spent years of selfish wandering, greedy for reward and personal gain to the detriment of those around you. At the Sanctuary of the Abbey, we learn to look within ourselves to find how we can truly help others."

Mother Pascal stood and, with the taller man, walked over to Charlotte, who was becoming more and more uncomfortable.

"This is no sanctuary! This is... just fucking ridiculous!"

Charlotte was thrown onto the chair, which wobbled precariously. In a white fury, she broke away from the man and stood up face to face with Pascal, who was now upon her.

"How dare you?!" she shouted.

Without a word, Mother Pascal's gnarled hand slapped Charlotte hard across the face.

In utter bewilderment, Charlotte stared at her attacker. Her hand moved to her burning cheek.

"At the Abbey, we believe in selflessness," the man who held her whispered, "Your ego repulses them."

Chapter 4

Being rudely woken and frog-marched to the meeting room at daybreak had not improved Pat's mood. She would happily have foregone breakfast to puff on a Marlboro, and the stupidly pretty roommate with her slender hips and porcelain skin irritated Pat further. She had wished for a kindred spirit, not a Big Brother bimbo.

"Pat, take a chair."

"I need a cigarette."

"Take a chair, Pat."

"I need a cigarette then I'll take a chair."

There was a sigh and a mutter, "Just give her a cigarette, or she won't bloody cooperate."

The cigarette was produced, Pat took a chair. The transformation was miraculous.

"What can I do for you, gentlemen?" she purred.

"There are changes this year, Pat. The funding has increased. Stramford's meeting with the PM went favourably, and we're expanding."

"Expanding how?" Pat knitted her brows.

"The facilities, generally, nothing you need to worry about. The numbers remain the same. The morphine supply is good. The PM's boy needs more help."

The speaker was a bespectacled man in his late fifties; his hair was dappled grey, and he had crinkles about the eyes that gave his face a warmth.

"Where does that new girl fit in?"

"She needs work and some gentle conditioning. She's no use to anyone at the moment."

Pat nodded gently, enjoying the cigarette. She rolled the papery thing between her thumb and forefinger.

"Tell me," she said, "What made this girl such a snob? She 'as a pretty face an' there's somethin' nice in her manner, but Jesus, don't she think she's somethin' special?"

The suits conferred but left Pat's question hanging in the air. Unperturbed, Pat continued to smoke as she watched them passing papers amongst themselves, discussing things she was not a party to, until finally, Pat was given something to sign.

"So, what's in it for me, gentlemen? Where's my cake? I never had to babysit a red shirt before. Usually, they're pretty biddable. This one ain't. She'll be a right handful."

The tallest of the suits, by the name of Mr Wilks, stepped forward towards Pat's chair. He crouched with one hand clamped around the plastic armrest, the heavily jawed face level with Pat's.

"Too much of a handful, you say?"

His cologne stung her nostrils and mixed with the last wisps of the cigarette. His face was so close that she could see the pores across his nose. Pat looked away and clenched her dentures together. Suddenly, taking her finished cigarette from her fingers, he threw it to the floor. Straightening up, he crushed it under his foot.

"Put that in the bin when you leave," he said as she stared at the flattened remains.

"Is that clear then, Pat?" came the voice of the original speaker, "You reinforce everything she gets; you're in the same boat as her. You're messed up, bored and seeking a spiritual path, right? Answer her questions, encourage her to accept the system readily."

"And when do I get me cigarettes back?"

The suits left and stole across the corridor towards the praise group. Mr Wilks walked over to the group of workmen and pulled out a large tablet. The high-vis jackets gathered around him and discussions began. There was a whiteboard above the table, and drawings emerged with measurements. A few nods, a short outbreak of laughter and a conclusive handshake.

Wilks then walked with the tablet towards the three who had gone into one of the medical rooms. A delivery of boxes was being wheeled from the double doors to a large storage room, and the tallest man was giving further instructions. They bore the mark of medical supplies, though no further clue as to their specific use was evident.

Several red-shirted women walked through the corridors, some carrying cleaning or medical equipment. Mr Wilks whistled one over and crouched to speak quietly in her ear. She nodded obediently and went off towards the cabins.

"Are you okay Charlotte?"

Chapter 5

Charlotte groaned and turned to the direction of the voice.

"I've brought you some tea... and toast if you want it," the voice trailed off, "You know it will get easier... things are going to get better."

Charlotte opened her eyes. By her bedside was sister Bernadine, her face etched with concern.

"The pain will subside quickly... there's no lasting damage."

Charlotte felt a tingling sensation on her face and could almost trace the hand of Mother Pascal upon her cheek.

"Why am I back here? What the hell has happened to me?" Charlotte's eyes flicked across to the other bed; it was empty.

"Where's that lady Pat? Why's she not in her bed? I need my phone. I have to phone my dad. Do you know what... what has just happened to me?"

"Yes. I know."

"How?"

"It happens to all of us, Charlotte."

"What?"

She turned to the young sister.

"It happens to all of us. It is the way in which we purify our souls before God..."

"Sister Bernadine... are you actually fucking serious?" Charlotte looked straight into her eyes.

"Charlotte... I know it seems so strange, but... but you have to trust me."

"You mean to say those.... those animals down there go about intimidating and forcing religion upon people... to heal them!? We're not in the bloody dark ages!"

Sister Bernadine smiled.

"But... but Charlotte. Do you not feel... Do you not feel better? Do you not feel a sense of relief?"

"Good God..." Charlotte mumbled and drew aside the covers.

She sat up but felt a strange dizziness.

"Have I been drugged or something?!"

"Charlotte, I'm only asking you to hear me out. You have no reason to distrust me. I am like you. I am more like you than you know."

Pulling herself out of bed with a cry, Charlotte began a frantic scramble for her clothes. Finding nothing but the establishment red shirt and jeans, she put them on, ran her fingers clumsily through her hair and pulled it into a loose tail.

"This place is a bloody lunatic asylum!"

Shoving her socked feet into the cheap plastic sandals that had presumably been put out for her, she made for the door.

"Charlotte, will you just listen to me?"

"No! You're as nuts as the rest of them!" with that, she threw open the door.

Running with some difficulty across the gardens, she felt her throat constrict with the cold air. Contrary to her slim athletic build, Charlotte was not particularly fit. Gasping uncomfortably, she slowed to a brisk walk. Reaching the end of the old graveyard, she hopped easily over the low wall that marked the boundary. She was now walking through longish grass which swished against her socks. The sandals, though comfortable, were not in any way protective against the dew.

Casting several glances behind her, she half expected to see the four suited men charging up, with the deranged Mother Pascal... along with some nuns perhaps, though nuns weren't in the habit of running, were they? Charlotte found herself smiling at the Monty Python-style vision conjured. Tearing her thoughts away, she looked ahead. She could see the first of the great line of oak trees and the cobbled road that would take her to the great iron gates. Quickening her pace, she broke into a jog. The sun was starting to slice through the cold morning, and Charlotte welcomed its warmth.

She looked behind again and felt a strange disappointment that still no pursuers had appeared. Could they not send some of those red-shirted folk, at least? Was she not important enough to chase after?

Charlotte stopped completely. The beautiful oak trees released their bronze leaves in confetti flurries while a squirrel broke free from a branch and bounded across to the next tree. There was a dappled piece of sunlight illuminating an old tree stump. Charlotte wandered over and, after a tentative feel of its mossy surface, had a seat. Still, no one came. She watched ladybirds walking up the highest blades of grass, opening their scarlet wingcase and taking off. There were autumnal wildflowers everywhere, yellow wispy ones with tiny delicate petals. There were the richest blues, pinks, oranges and reds. A mighty bumble bee wobbled noisily about, comically buffeting the flowers about with its huge furry body.

"You're a bit late, aren't you, matey?" she chuckled, "Aren't you supposed to be hibernating at this time of year?"

Charlotte looked back again, with less urgency this time. She thought no one would come. She didn't care if they did either; she just wanted to enjoy this lovely, peaceful moment.

Casting her mind back, trying to conjure up the last time she sat blissfully surrounded by nature like this. She couldn't. This was something rare and private. Had she not yearned for something like this when her dad finally, after a long reproachful stare, said, "You need to get yourself sorted, love. You're a mess."

After a long and lovely time, Charlotte noticed with dismay that there were two figures heading towards her, though they were still a considerable distance away. With a sigh, she left the tree stump and took up a fast walk alongside the oaks. The sun shone down, and soon, the cool relief of the oaks was replaced with glaring light, which slowed her to an amble. She felt weak, and the elation of the countryside was quickly being replaced with foreboding.

She stopped and turned round. The figures were gaining on her, though they didn't move aggressively. Tired and defeated, Charlotte turned and walked slowly towards the shady tree trunk.

'I'll hear them out, politely decline their loony bin course of redemption and be on my bloody way... tonight,' she thought, with private defiance. 'Meantime...' the inner dialogue continued, 'I'm going to enjoy this sunshine, the flowers and the sodding bees.'

A small smile reached her lips. The little bit of drama, the run across the countryside, the sheer different-ness of it all had felt weirdly good, almost invigorating.

"Charlotte?"

Charlotte turned to see Bernadine and another young woman in a red polo shirt. She was of mixed race, strikingly beautiful and unusually tall.

"Charlotte, this is Jasmine. Can we talk? Can you hear us out?"

"No, I've talked enough. I need my phone. I need to leave this place."

Charlotte, you cannot leave. You do not exist in your old life anymore. You have to understand that you are here to stay."

A big disbelieving smile cracked across Charlotte's face.

"Pardon?"

"I'm not joking, Charlotte. You are in something bigger than you can understand at the moment."

"Can you quit the patronising 'not understanding' theme? How about you... both, explain clearly what you're on about, then with any luck, I will understand..." she rolled the word out sarcastically, "and then I can get the fuck home."

Jasmine bristled, almost fearfully, and kept looking back from where they had come.

She said in a low voice, "Charlotte, you gotta listen up. It's better to hear from us now. You will adjust fine. You just need to understand the situation you're in."

Bees and insects continued to buzz, unperturbed by the strange tension that was building amongst the young women. The trees danced about as the lightest of breezes ruffled their remaining leaves.

"This place is a fully realised concept of a very powerful man. Edward Stramford. We believe he may be a prince or royalty, at least. He holds influence in the British government and has huge accumulated wealth. He has the financial power to do anything he likes."

"Anything he likes?" parroted Charlotte with her mouth straight but her eyes still in disbelief.

"You don't need to know that, but it's worth knowing." Jasmine paused, looking at Bernadine, who nodded faintly.

"This place was set up to keep people, to keep people who were a... nuisance. To keep them safe..."

"To care for them... and attend to their needs," chipped in Bernadine.

"Who? Who's a nuisance? Am I a nuisance? To whom?"

"No, let's not talk about you... This place was set up with a huge amount of funding. As well as the Abbey itself, there are gardens, riding stables, a gym, a library, all to mock 'real life' but within the confines of the walls," Jasmine paused and looked briefly over her shoulder.

Satisfied that they were alone, she continued, "It's designed to give people who have been a nuisance to society a place to live out contented lives where they will not cause problems for powerful connections they have in the 'real world.'"

"Like who? What do you mean?"

"Ok... say there was a princess... who strayed from her prince. Say she misbehaved, made a nuisance of herself and brought down the family name in full view of the public. That behaviour would not... do; therefore, she would inadvertently be heading for the Abbey."

"Ok, so what, do they pack the princess into a car and drive her around without anyone batting an eyelid? You don't think the public would miss her?"

"That's where the muscular arm of the Abbey flexes."

Jasmine knelt on the grass by Charlotte's tree stump. Bernadine continued to stand though her hands were clasped together, and the knuckles shone oddly white.

"The princess meets with an accident; God help her," Bernadine whispered.

The whole accident is orchestrated with top military precision. Evidence is collected swiftly and efficiently. Even high-ranking police detectives are unknowingly complicit. The family is told that the death certificate is signed, and sleek as you like, a car rolls up this very road with the naughty princess inside.

Jasmine adjusted herself on the long grass so that she could keep half an eye on the Abbey. The jeans were too short for her long legs and revealed strong calves.

"Ok, so I'm in an institution for naughty princesses? Not a nunnery and most definitely not a Spa?" rebuffed Charlotte.

"We are all here for similar reasons. You are obviously connected to someone who is highly influential or wealthy. Yet you're not important enough to be looked after as such... you're like Bernadine, me and the other red shirts. We have to provide care."

"Or what?"

"I really wouldn't keep up that defensive stance much longer. You've got it lucky being able to talk to us first. Many didn't, and they went mad or were beaten half to death through their own... stupidity."

Jasmine's eyes glazed over, and she looked away.

With a step closer, Bernadine interjected, "The chapel is there for you, Charlotte. It's there for all of us. If we seek to please God, our lives will have true meaning by serving all the residents here. We are serving God."

Charlotte scoffed, "Save that shit... save it. Why are you both here? I can't leave then, right? That's what you're saying? I have to work? I have to be one of those helpers with the Praise group?"

Charlotte dismounted the tree stump and started towards the boundary but stopped.

"What's going to happen if I make a bid to escape then? I now see what that flipping wall with its razor wire is about. It's not to keep people out but to keep people in!"

Bernadine began to speak but stopped short as she looked out towards the Abbey. Someone was coming.

"Charlotte, there's no time. I wish we had more time."

Her eyes looked desperate.

"The praise group are just the same as the others... they're considered to be a burden, so they're sent here... They have wealthy connections, so they're kept alive... and happy... they're happy, but Charlotte, promise me one thing. Please?"

Bernadine and Jasmine had found each other and had linked arms. Jasmine's demeanour was stiffening with every approaching footstep of the figure. Charlotte, some metres away from them, took a step closer.

"What is it?" she almost whispered, sobered by their altered faces.

"You must do as you're told. You must not be defiant."

The two women stood motionless with their eyes downcast but for their hair, which gently danced about in the breeze. Charlotte moved two steps closer to form a triangle, a strange sort of comradeship emanating from the shape. With a hand to her brow, she squinted through the sun at the approaching figure. It was a tall and bearded man. He wore a dark expensive- looking suit. When upon the trio, he stopped.

"Sister Bernadine, Sister Jasmine."

"Mr Wilks."

They both dipped into a small curtsey and at once moved swiftly away back towards the Abbey.

"You are to go with them," he spoke with authority.

Chapter 6

Two uniformed police officers stepped back as the large entrance gates opened. A black Bentley with darkened windows swept smoothly up the long driveway towards the elegant line of oaks. Inside the car was a smartly dressed couple. The Nigerian man had large, powerful shoulders; his hand rested protectively on his wife's thigh as she looked out and away from him through the trees and towards the approaching Abbey. She was petite with chestnut hair swept elegantly into a bun. Her skin was pale, as if she had never seen the sun. In sharp contrast, she had a smear of strong red lipstick, which matched the rubies that dangled from her ears. The smartly suited driver kept his eyes firmly on the road.

Two suits stepped out of the main front door and stood to welcome in the car. The taller suit, Mr Wilks, checked his watch and straightened his cufflinks. There was the faint sound of a tennis game at the courts behind the Abbey. Small red dots of the polo-shirted staff could be seen in the gardens as the sun shone gloriously down. A light breeze ruffled the browning leaves from the climbers that hung across the cemetery entrance as the car pulled to a stop.

The driver hopped out and pulled open the door for the lady. The couple walked to the two suited men who extended their hands and greeted them with warm smiles. Small talk was exchanged about the weather and their health, and soon, they were climbing the wide steps through the threshold.

"Prime Minister, Lady Nkosi, I wonder if I can interest you in a short tour around the facilities before we visit your son. I believe Michael may well be enjoying his lunch as we speak."

"Mr Compton, is it? Or are you Mr Wilks? I apologise. I don't believe we have met in person," smiled the Nigerian.

"I'm Bill, Bill Compton. Of course, though we've communicated online many times, I have not had the pleasure," he extended his hand, which was accepted warmly.

"And the tour is fine, though it's short, yes? My wife is tired and would like to see Michael sooner rather than later."

Mr Compton nodded and took the couple through the bright hallway towards the abbey. The small party was met by Mother Pascal at the ornate Abbey doors, and she and Mrs Nkosi broke away slightly from the men. There was instant recognition and tangible relief in the prime minister's wife as she took the arm of Mother Pascal like an old friend.

"Oh, Heather, I've been so anxious about this. Isn't that just so silly?"

"Not a bit," Mother Pascal replied warmly.

"I don't want to overwhelm you with praise, but I truly believe both you and Mr Nkosi are pioneers of change,

51

ensuring the absolute best outcomes for both your child and the country as a whole."

Lady Nkosi smiled, showing beautifully straight teeth, though the smile didn't quite reach her eyes.

"Forgive my directness," continued the taller lady, "but I believe it can only be selfish to restrict the potential of special young people by claiming them as possessions. Michael is happier every time I see him. He has friends, and he has so many things to do here..."

"And his pains? How are his pains?"

"He uses a steady programme of morphine, it is painless, and we have now developed a liquid form which is as pleasant as the miraculous pink... Calpol!"

"Oh, that really is splendid. He always liked Calpol. I understand he is not... he is not being treated anymore. The morphine is purely for pain relief."

"It is God's way, and although he is weak, we will ensure that his journey to Heaven is as smooth and painless as one could wish for."

A quartet of red shirts filed into the Abbey and stood in front of the choir stalls. They held a black hymn book, each in perfect unison. They opened their books and looked out across the guests to the stained-glass window. The chair by the organ creaked as an elderly man sat and began thumbing through his music.

"Let's not wait a moment longer. I'm going to take you to see him now. Will your husband be happy to continue the tour in your absence?"

"Oh, I'm sure he'll be fine."

Lady Nkosi had already turned her back and was heading for the door as Mother Pascal quickly briefed Bill Compton. Both men were deep in discussion, and it appeared to the Prime minister's wife that her husband was much more interested in the Abbey than in their son.

"They are eighteen and above. It just cannot be put through legally if they're minors... Oh, absolutely, we've tried... McCannon and Proctor spent years on it..."

Mr Compton's voice lingered in an echo before being silenced by the thud of the door. The two ladies walked along the path of the old cemetery. Lady Nkosi's eyes flitted from one headstone to the next. She tilted her head away from the stones and up to the trees overhead, where hidden birds chirruped joyfully.

"Michael will be twenty-three next month... the doctors didn't think he'd make it into adulthood you know... he was always so small, so delicate."

Mother Pascal nodded and allowed the smaller woman to continue.

"I think I would have killed him eventually... or myself."

There were tears bulging threateningly at her eyelashes. Reaching into her handbag, the lady took a folded tissue and, without unfolding it, neatly drained the corners of both eyes, in a way which suggested she was well used to saving her makeup.

"I had to administer so many damn medicines... the poor child would look with such horror at me... oh, I hated it... Heather, I hated him. I hated my own son."

Heather Pascal put a hand on her shoulder.

"It is these times that we look to Jesus when we think God has forsaken us, we look to Jesus, brutalised and nailed to the cross, and we know that God has a higher plan than we can ever comprehend."

Lady Nkosi fumbled in her handbag and produced a small bottle and a mirror. She sprayed a fine mist over her face, patted her hair and quickly applied a fresh coat of lipstick.

Mr Compton and Mr Bim Nkosi were joined by the tallest suit, Mr Wilks, by the time they got round to the tennis courts. Nkosi had found the sensory garden playful and clever with its use of running water for both visual and auditory effects. The topiarised hedges that surrounded it were so astonishingly precise that he joked whether the gardeners lived within the garden itself for fear a leaf would blow untidily across the grass. The suits laughed appreciatively and were anxious to impress him. They further shared gallant tales of the lengths gone to ensure the garden was just so. Legendary names were dropped here and there, such as sons of princes, daughters of wealthy bankers, and wives of powerful sheikhs.

"Years ago, a Middle Eastern gentleman tried to dump three of his wives here in one go at the whim of his remaining wife, who was jealous of the others. They were clawing at each other's eyes in a rage even he had never seen!" chuckled Compton.

"The tennis courts are splendid," asserted Bim Nkosi, "I've not seen finer than these even in Brisbane."

His eyes scoured the tree line.

"Even your floodlights are an artistic statement," he chuckled and loosened his tie a little, "Where next, gentlemen? Please lead on."

The paintings in the corridor were ugly, and Mrs Nkosi had to pull her eyes away from them for fear that her lip would curl in distaste. She did not want to appear callous and had taken several private deep breaths so as to compose herself further.

Mother Pascal opened the door, which held the 'Praise Group' placard. Inside were 3 pleasant-looking ladies, all in matching red polo shirts. They were all busy preparing craft and painting equipment. One blonde middle-aged lady was by the sink rinsing brushes and plastic beakers. A Chinese woman with the most beautiful thick, shiny plait over her shoulder was writing names in marker pen on the bottom corners of drying splodgy paintings. The third woman was much older than the others, with short grey hair. She moved to greet them.

"Lady Nkosi, this is Patricia. I expect you remember Pat from last time?"

Mrs Nkosi offered her hand and politely nodded at the other two ladies who were looking over with interest. She looked at the paintings and smiled at the plaited woman.

"These are cheerful pictures, are they not?"

"Yes, Madam."

"Come, let's make haste and see Michael before nap time."

Mother Pascal motioned Mrs Nkosi to follow her through to the next room. This room was replete with sofas and beanbags. There was a TV affixed to the wall playing silent cartoons. There was one section of the wall that was papered entirely with colourful spots like large smarties, and the cushions that peppered the sofas all matched. It felt innocent and childlike, aside from the mobility aids that were tucked close to the sofas, just within sight.

"Michael's through 'ere," Pat said, beckoning the small party through, "He likes the peace of 'is bedroom after lunch."

A boy-sized figure sat on a large double bed, but wizened and sad-looking. His afro hair was cut smartly, and he wore a hooded jumper with stripes down each arm. He had a games console in one hand, yet he appeared to be lost in thought. His eyes flicked over to Pat, and recognition swept over his face, but almost as soon, it was replaced by suspicion.

"What, Pat?"

"There there, love, it ain't anythin' different to normal love. It's yer mammy's come to see you."

Pat moved to his side, arm around his thin shoulders.

"Ye've got that picture to show yer mammy, ain't ye love? Where'd you put it, hey?"

The small figure sprang up from the bed, and out of Pat's grasp. Marching straight over to his mother, he began pounding her with his small fists. Without knowing what to do, she pushed him gently away, back towards the bed.

"It's me, darling. It's mummy."

Michael ran over to Pat, who crouched to meet his eyes.

"It's yer mammy Michael, she's 'ere to see you."

"I brought you something, Michael," Mrs Nkosi said, unclipping her handbag.

She pulled out a small paper bag and handed it to Pat.

"Now, what's this then love? There's somethin' for you here."

Michael peered towards the bag in Pat's hand but did not reach over.

"Shall I open it for ye love?"

A small metal car was lifted out of the bag. Pat carefully placed it in Michael's hand, taking care to wrap his fingers around it as if he would drop it. He closed his eyes as if concentrating. His fingers found the small silver wheels and turned them. He brought it close to his face and opened his eyes. A crooked grin reached his mouth.

Mother Pascal, who had remained silent, stepped further into the room.

"That's a lovely choice of gift, Lady Nkosi. I do believe he likes it!"

Michael's head snapped up as if noticing the large nun for the first time.

A low growl began to gather deep within the boy as his brows furrowed.

"Mother Pascal, dear Lady Nkosi. I think 'es a bit tired now. Perhaps you might like a... refreshment break?" Pat glanced quickly at Michael.

"No, I am quite refreshed, thank you. I travelled a rather long way to see Michael and..."

Without warning, there was a sharp bang as the small car ricocheted off the wall. Lady Nkosi let out a small scream. The scream was dwarfed by a strange howl that erupted from her son. The whole torso of the young man shook with the effort of such projection, and his expression was wracked with a crazed despair.

Pat tried again, "Ladies, I really think Michael would be better alone for a bit, just to 'ave a bit of a nap. It's a lot for 'im to take in."

Lady Nkosi, though visibly shaken, remained in the room.

"He is my son! I will not be forced away from him."

Blinking away unwanted tears, she began to move purposely towards Michael. He had slumped to a kneel, though his back stayed rigid. His eyes spun furiously from his mother to Pat... his mother... Pat. Reaching out, Lady Nkosi took her son's shoulder.

He hissed.

She whipped her hand back as if scalded.

"Well gentlemen, I think it safe to say you have a smooth system running here. I would appreciate a return visit in the not-too-distant future."

Prime Minister Nkosi had taken off his blazer and loosened his tie since his exertions on the tennis courts. His wrist twinged slightly, reminding him that it had been a while since his last game.

"You'll need to come prepared for doubles next time, sir!" quipped Mr Compton.

"Well Bill, I hope you've a good partner, if you've even a hope of success."

The two men clapped backs and chuckled, both content to cool down with a beer and a meander around the gardens. Two young ladies in red polo shirts walked smartly over to the three gentlemen, took the Prime Minister's jacket and offered a tray of ice-cold beers.

"Sure you're not wanting a seat Mr Nkosi? There's a beautiful seating area near to the paddocks."

"You know, Mr Compton, I find that sitting often snubs my mood. I associate sitting with meetings, and it's rarer for me to be out of them than in."

"Quite."

The three men, beer in hand, began a slow amble away from the tennis courts and towards the stables and paddocks.

"So tell me, Mr Wilks, as my terminally ill son declines in health, how will you keep me informed of his progress?"

"However often and in whatever form you should wish, sir."

"I understand that he is to be looked after, though not treated, as such. Mr Wilks?"

"Indeed, sir, the Abbey holds firm in its assertion that prolonging the lives of those who suffer cannot be in their best interests. Rather, we believe in a whole and rich life experience right until it cannot be sustained."

"Indeed."

"If there is no joy in life, it must be allowed to naturally extinguish so that the soul can be liberated, sir. Of course, at the Abbey, this process ensures dignity and comfort to the very end."

"It is the best way," the Nigerian agreed, though his shoulders slouched slightly.

"You know, gentlemen, I wish that my own father was afforded such a dignified death as you describe. It is inhumane to allow such suffering in old age as well as illness, and we call ourselves civilised? Hah!"

The three men had stopped their slow amble by a shaded area near the stables. Men in red polo shirts were busy in the yard pushing wheelbarrows, sweeping and lifting heavy hay bales.

"Yes... yes, it's a smooth system running here," mused the Nigerian as he drained his glass.

Chapter 7

For two long weeks, Charlotte had been either locked in her cabin or set to work in the stables or kitchens. The first outing to the stables had resulted in a failed escape attempt. Two of the men working in the yard had accosted her by the oak trees and all but dragged her kicking and screaming back to the yard. They did not throw her into her cabin as she had supposed they would, but to her surprise, they handed her a heavy broom and pushed her towards the stable entrance.

No one seemed particularly interested in the mistreatment she had received, how much she missed her possessions, particularly her phone, or how stupid this whole institution was. Only the horses followed her movements under their long eyelashes as their glossy heads leaned out of the stables. One particular horse, black as ebony with a long pretty mane, would toss its head when she came near and occasionally whinny as if in recognition. Charlotte supposed she must look like its owner, having never ridden a horse in her life.

In the early days, she approached the great animal very cautiously. By day three of working at the stables, she had plucked up the courage to rub her hand on its velvety nose and was delighted when the huge animal, with both ears forward, put its large head cradled within her arms.

One sunny morning, as Charlotte got to work clearing the third of the seven stables, she paused to kick straw out of the regulation sandals she had to wear. She had already raised a sweat, forking manure away from one corner of the stable and piling it up in her wheelbarrow. She was just on the point of fluffing up the remaining straw when a shadow appeared at the door frame. It was Mr Wilks. He had to stoop to enter the stable and, once inside, stood in such a manner as to block her in.

Holding his gaze, she awaited a greeting, but none came. She felt the cool metal handle of the fork in her right hand. It felt reassuring to have a potential weapon, though she did not feel bold. A strange quiet ensued as neither spoke for a number of seconds.

Finally unable to stand the silence, Charlotte broke, "Can I help you?"

He offered no response other than to continue to gaze at her with a darkening intensity.

Becoming increasingly uncomfortable, Charlotte raised her hand to wipe a single bead of sweat that had released itself from her hairline and was tickling its way toward her eyebrows. The movement seemed to spur Mr Wilks to motion, and taking his phone from his lapel pocket, he proceeded to open a document and enlarge it so he could read the small text. Transferring his weight from one leg to the other, he continued to read from his phone, scrolling down and zooming in, scrolling and zooming.

Charlotte felt trapped, but she was armed. There wasn't any immediate danger, though she felt indecisive. Should she continue fluffing up the straw regardless of the tall man invading her space, or should she stand to attention as so many of the other red shirts seemed to do? With a cautious step away from the door and back into the stable, Charlotte began gently forking the top layer of the straw. Tension grew tangibly in the air. Charlotte could feel the gaze of the man who had moved from his phone to her.

Clearing his throat, he spoke, "You are to attend a meeting and will be collected at the refectory after lunch."

"Why?"

"Why?" repeating her word, he watched her closely.

Raising a hand to his bristled cheek, he scratched thoughtfully.

"I want to know where my phone is... I need to contact my family... I'm due to go home soon," Charlotte stammered, heart hammering.

Surely, he would have a heart; if not, he definitely wouldn't risk a fork through his skull.

"You do not leave the Abbey until you have been released. That is, of course... if you are released at all."

His beard twitched to reveal a thin smile before continuing, "You have had an education, though it would seem you squandered it. You have been sent here to be cured. Of course, as you will know so well, the intentions of those around you hardly matter; it is only you who can save yourself."

Suddenly, longing to be out of his shadow, beyond the stable and galloping across the long grass, she blurted out, "Can I use another phone then? What about your phone? Can I use that?"

"Idiot," Mr Wilkes growled, replacing his phone in his pocket.

With a last intense look, he turned and strode out of the stable towards the Abbey.

Bernadine and Jasmine came to collect Charlotte for lunch as they always did. While Charlotte had been working at the stables, Bernadine and Jasmine were with the other nuns at choir practice and Bible study. After lunch, Charlotte would be sent to the kitchens to wash up, prepare salads, clean and be a general dogsbody where required. The chef, Mr Romano, was a small but impressively inflated Italian man, so emotional was he that his large belly would shudder from tears, laughter, or outbursts of song as he bellowed commands to his staff. Even though they implied they were terrified of the eccentric chef, they all knew beneath the caricatured exterior, that he was both sensitive and kind.

Today, though, Charlotte would not be carted off to the kitchen, and Mr Romano would have to take his chopping boards to another red shirt to wash.

"How's your morning been, Charlotte?" Jasmine asked cheerfully.

"Ok, all ok. I had a visit from Mr Wilks, though. In the stable over there," Charlotte casually threw a thumb behind her, "He wants me to meet him... them... someone, after lunch. What do you think he wants Jasmine? Are they going to ask me to redeem myself before God again?"

Bernadine winced but said nothing.

Jasmine replied, "I don't know Charlotte... I'd like to help prepare you a bit if I can. Maybe they're going to give you more permanent roles here. That's what happened to me a couple of weeks in. Yes, maybe you'll get a timetable or something."

The three walked away from the fields and were now on the outskirts of the tennis courts. A mixed doubles game was going on, but the three young women paid no heed. Bernadine placed her hand on Charlotte's shoulder.

"If you are to go through the next stage of redemption, Charlotte, I can only implore you to reach out to God. Fighting against his love will do you no good if you are to flourish here. If it's too much to begin with, then spend some time at the chapel for quiet reflection. It will enable you to understand what is happening around you."

Charlotte rolled her eyes. It was rude, and she knew it. She felt utterly compelled to shake her sweet little companion by the shoulders and tell her to get a grip.

Swallowing back her unkind thoughts, she turned to Bernadine and, with a smile, said, "I'll try."

The meal was conducted in silence, as always; the shepherd's pie —plain and lacking salt— and the vegetables —overcooked. It was unusual for the food to be substandard, and Charlotte wondered if Mr Romano was ill or had taken an emotional episode in the kitchen.

As the red shirts, and then the nuns, filed quietly out of the refectory, Charlotte sat still, awaiting instructions for Mr Wilk's meeting. Her bench, by design, turned her back to the dining hall, and the space opposite was now vacant. The plates had been cleared, the cups gone, the tables wiped. Only a faint line of crumbs remained where the cloth had missed. Charlotte looked at the small line and counted 6 small crumbs, 5 tiny white ones and 1 larger orange one. They sat in a groove of the wood grain. The orange one might be the teacher, the five white ones, little pupils.

BANG!

A hand slammed down upon the table. The crumbs scattered.

"Oh!" In shock, Charlotte threw up her hands and immediately stood to face whatever had startled her.

It was Pat, grinning away.

"C'mon love, what yu daydreamin' about?!" Charlotte felt her heart race, and she took a breath.

"Pat, you bloody startled me. God! My heart's going like the clappers."

"Sorry love, couldn't resist. Are you tired? You're s'posed to be 'eading over to the Stramford room with me. We've got a meeting, apparently. Know what it's about?"

"No."

"Desperate for a cig, I wish you smoked, you useless... You could've covered for me while I 'ad a little check in Wilk's office."

"You don't actually take his cigarettes, do you?!" Charlotte couldn't believe the guts of this older woman.

"Na... they ration them out to me like I'm some kind of flippin' pet. I'm seriously considering it, though, love. Wilks puffs away on them Marlboro like a bloody chimney."

Charlotte walked with Pat out of the refectory and down the corridor, passing the praise room and finding the door with the carved placard.

Pat hung back just a little and whispered, "After you love."

Charlotte knocked tentatively. The door was too heavy to give clues as to who was inside or what they were saying. After a few moments, Pat reached past Charlotte and rapped the door assertively.

"Enter."

The two women stepped inside, and the door closed quietly behind them. A circular oak meeting table had four filled and three vacant chairs. Mr Wilks motioned for the ladies to sit. To the right of Mr Wilks sat Mother Pascal. A bearded man sat to her left, and finally, there was a man of Indian descent.

Mother Pascal spoke first.

"Ladies, it has come to my attention that there have been some issues arising from a number of acts of defiance from you both. Although this is not altogether unusual for our newer residents, we have found from experience that it is often best to allow grievances to be shared so that we can all work together for common goals, such as productivity, discipline and ultimately, a shared peace."

She paused to take a small sip of water from a tumbler, "In the two weeks you have been here, you will have pieced together an idea of what the Abbey is about, what it offers and how you fit into its system. You will be aware that the

Abbey thrives on a hierarchy that enables the smooth running of this establishment and results in the best possible outcomes for all who reside here. You will have to adapt away from many of your badly ingrained behaviours, such as selfishness, assertiveness and greed."

"I didn't ask to come here!" Charlotte suddenly blurted out.

"No one asks to exist at all. No baby chooses its parents or their circumstances; they cry for milk and warmth with equal need, whether they're babes of royalty or beggars. You, Charlotte Compton, have arrived at an establishment that ensures your every need is met with professional sensitivity and dignity. The world you have left is driven by monetary gain alone. Depravity, greed, unkindness and worst of all... purposelessness are rife in a world where religion is obsolete. Here in the Abbey, you will discover your potential not only to maximise your abilities but to help others. Something I suspect you have long failed to do."

Charlotte sneaked a quick look at Pat, who sat motionless, eyes ahead.

"This is the opportunity for you both to ask any questions you may have so that there is no ambiguity as to expectations of behaviour."

Mother Pascal rose and walked to the back of the room, pulled open the drawer of an ornately carved cabinet and took out two stapled books of paper. They were handed to both Pat and Charlotte.

"In this booklet, the expectations of the Abbey are clearly outlined. You are to fulfil all tasks without complaint, and you will find a reward such as the increase of your freedom to use the wide-ranging facilities here."

Charlotte flicked through the pages of the thick pamphlet. She saw bullet points, a number of diagrams and photographs of the facilities.

"I am expected to become a nun by the end of my stay? I'm not religious. I don't believe in any of it."

Charlotte looked straight into the eyes of Mother Pascal, remembering the crack of her hand across her jaw.

"That is one of the very first points of correction, to become a selfless disciple. Many aspire to reach such spiritual heights, but you, with your life of shameless navel gazing and consumerism, will struggle to overcome this particular hurdle. We are not here to educate you; you've been through school and university. The resources here are extensive and very much available to you. The Abbey is a great machine, and you are a cog. In time, you will understand your place".

"Cogs can be replaced," interjected the Indian man, "It is in your best interest to keep yourself productive and pleasant so as not to beckon replacement too soon."

Pat, who had sat unnaturally still, finally adjusted herself slightly in her seat.

"Well, that sounds dead clear to me."

Charlotte turned to Pat in disbelief, "You're joking, right? We've just been informed that we're effectively incarcerated in this place for God knows how long, and you're just going to accept it like that?!"

Charlotte stood, scraping her chair noisily as she rose, but was greatly surprised that in a matter of seconds, she was physically forced down in her seat again by one of the men who had so politely held open the door as they entered.

"Temper tantrums are not tolerated here, Charlotte. Your aggressive outbursts will be met with equal violence until you learn to control yourself and speak in a civilised manner," Mother Pascal's voice was low and assertive.

"As I said, you will have to unlearn your bad habits as they will be tolerated less and less. It would be wise for you to study the booklet in your hand so as to be clear about our expectations. You are no better than anyone here. We are all God's children."

Pat turned to Charlotte with a flicker of sympathy in her eyes but turned almost immediately to the front again. The man who had put Charlotte back in her seat had disappeared back to the door.

"This is ludicrous!" Charlotte tailed her words off, waiting for an angry retort, but when none came, she continued, " I'm to stay here for the rest of my life, clearing stables and washing dishes? I'm a musician. I spent years of study to... to... to perform."

The Indian man spoke softly, "You never really have performed though, have you? You cancelled again and again. Even though you were given everything you could wish for, you were lazy and churlish. All the investment in you and your voice came to nothing. Not because you didn't possess the raw talent, you did. It was because you couldn't be bothered. You wanted to go out with your friends and get hopelessly drunk, so your father, time and time again, would have to clear up the pieces and cancel your shows."

"How would you know that?" Charlotte's eyes opened wide in disbelief.

"Is that why I'm here then? Dad's ultimate revenge?"

"Your father rose to success, against all the odds, through hard work and determination. An alcoholic mother and father died in the war. All his siblings were stuck on the gruelling treadmill of modern life, and your father, Charlotte, studied at night school and took himself all the way up to a top ministerial position in the British Government. Even with your mother dying of cancer at such a young age, your father tirelessly worked to keep you in the best schools in London. What a privileged upbringing you

73

had, but you thought you were better. You weren't grateful. You indecisively hopped from art school to music to performing arts, and when the work got tough, you got lazy."

"I'm not lazy."

"You finally went it alone, didn't you Charlotte? To prove to your father that you could do something by yourself. You failed at art school, wasted time at music college and finally decided to get a menial job and stand on your own two feet."

"Well, that took courage, didn't it?!"

"You broke your father's heart when you destroyed your bedroom in your London house in an almighty tantrum and marched out into the 'real world,' as you called it, to discover all the fun you had been missing. Off you went with a bank full of your father's money and bought yourself a house... and a car..."

"Well, how else could I get to work?!"

"A Porsche to get to work? Work at a high-end restaurant as a waitress. Tipped off by your concerned father, they took you in. Always late, never properly dressed, often rude. How long did you last there, Charlotte?"

"I dunno. A few months, maybe? It wasn't my fault. They were awful, the pay was bad, and they expected me to cover for the chambermaids in their absence. I'm not clearing hairs out of the God damn bath for a minimum bloody wage."

"Indeed, so you lost your job."

"As I said, it wasn't my fault."

"And you hung about with friends, sometimes singing in bars, mostly getting hopelessly drunk. Your father looking on in despair."

"Well, he should have sorted me out with a better job!"

"Should he?"

Charlotte gulped, "No, I... Oh, what?! What's the purpose of this?"

"The purpose of this is to allow you to understand that it is possible to redeem yourself of the sins of your past. We are all capable of change. You have been given a tremendous opportunity to give back all you have taken within the walls of the Abbey."

"So, what... what are you asking me to do?"

"You were briefly introduced to our Praise group on your first day. In addition to your kitchen and stable duties, which will continue, you will have a daily afternoon session working alongside the staff there, attending to the needs of the patients and carrying out the orders of the staff as required. Depending on how well you conduct yourself within the group, we will reflect upon your privileges in due course..."

The Indian man turned to Patricia and continued, "Pat, you will be working with the Praise group for slightly longer sessions and continuing your work in the kitchen. You have been dishonest with me about the cigarettes; therefore, you will spend one hour of daily reflection after dinner in the chapel."

"Yes, Sir."

Charlotte studied the panel closely. The Indian man looked familiar. Was he a friend of her father's? A government minister, perhaps. There had been a few sociable drinks gatherings at the house when Charlotte was young. She remembered hiding under the dinner table laden with canapes and wine. She marvelled at the polished shoes of all the guests, especially the women's elegant court shoes. She remembered her mother at the last stages of the cancer that had sabotaged her pretty face, making it puffy and yellow. Her feet no longer fitted into court shoes, only wide slippers in which she shuffled painfully from bed to bathroom. After her death came the sad, faraway look in her father's eyes as young Charlotte chatted to him about school.

Pulling herself away from painful memories, she looked at Mr Wilks, who met her eyes immediately with such intensity that Charlotte felt deeply uncomfortable. Pulling her eyes away from his gaze, she faced Mother Pascal.

"When do I leave here?"

"You will not leave."

"I bloody well WILL leave!" she stood abruptly and saw Pat put her hand to her forehead in disbelief.

Charlotte swung round, anticipating resistance from the man who had hauled her back into her seat earlier. He stood like an obedient soldier awaiting instructions.

"Charlotte, sit down."

"Let me go home!" Charlotte wailed as she stood awkwardly frozen.

"You are in no danger if you cooperate. Now sit down."

"You can't hold me here against my will. It's a basic human right to be free!" Charlotte barked the words at Mother Pascal with tears brimming in her eyes.

"Sit down."

"I want kids one day, a good job, I might marry. I can't stay here."

Charlotte stood shakily with one eye on the doorman.

"This is my last warning. Your disobedience will be met with equal violence until you learn to behave as a respectable citizen of this establishment. Tantrums are not tolerated; obedience is rewarded. You have the choice to follow a fulfilling path for yourself here by helping yourself and others. So, sit down."

"Charlotte, sit down for Chrissake!" hissed Pat from the corner of her mouth.

"No! No, Pat, I will NOT! Damn, the bloody lot of you!"

The doorman nodded to Mr Wilks and stepped towards Charlotte, pulling out a small black device from his pocket. Aiming it toward Charlotte, he looked again to Mr Wilks.

"Is that a taser?! Is that a taser gun? Good god!" with a spin, Charlotte threw herself into her chair and raised her hands above her.

"I'm sitting. I'm sitting."

Mr Wilks gave a tiny shake of the head to the doorman, who immediately retreated to the door with the taser device safely capped. The tears came then. Gushing down her face and dripping into her collar. Her back shuddered as she heaved great, sad sobs.

"The journey will be hard, my dear, but the destination will be greatly rewarding."

Mother Pascal took her leave, nodding politely to the doorman.

DOWNING STREET

Chapter 8

A solitary policeman stood guard outside the famous black door. To relieve the chill, he privately tensed and relaxed his muscles while pondering upon how many officers had stood feeling the cold outside this very door. The polished silver '10' shone like a mirror, the Victorian brass lion black in sharp contrast with the shiny gold letterbox. How many hands had turned that great brass handle? How many prime ministers and their wives, or indeed husbands, mused the man as he reflected on the few female ministers who achieved the top job.

A small number of reporters had gathered opposite, a short distance away, their trench coats flapped about as the brisk wind played. The ministerial cat trotted over, causing a minor stir with two of the women in particular. They stooped down to stroke it, and when they rose satisfied with their cat fix, the cat, still not content, walked neat figures of eight around as many legs as it could.

A loose newspaper sheet curved its spine and gathered the breeze underneath. Shaking in anticipation, it finally rose from the pavement, curling and opening, swooping like a tabloid butterfly.

The cat, startled by the foreign flying creature, arched its tabby back and felt the tingle down its spine as the fur stood up on end. One of the reporters absent-mindedly stooped to stroke the cat, who, frightened by the unexpected hand, propelled itself with such force across the forecourt that the policeman hastened to let the poor animal in.

"Tell me, Bim," remarked Pauline Nkosi as she sat on the edge of their satin-covered bed, gently loosening the gold strap on her shoe, "I've just been wondering how the Abbey ensures that the power imbalance that it seems to thrive on doesn't result in abuse."

"Power imbalance? I'm not sure what you mean. There's definitely a hierarchy within their system, but abuse? Of whom? Do you mean Michael?"

"No, I don't mean Michael. I know they work hard to ensure he's as happy as he can be. But I was thinking more widely."

She took both strappy shoes and neatly placed them by the foot of the bed.

Gently removing the rubies from her ears, she continued, "You're right to think I meant Michael, as he is very vulnerable, and of course, the most vulnerable in society are always targeted first. But I thought perhaps the staff as a whole, you know those red-shirted men and women that are dotted about everywhere, they run the gardens, the library, the gymnasium and so on."

"Did you see inside the gym, my dear? I stopped short at the indoor courts. They really are impressive."

The Prime Minister pulled off his blazer and put it on the back of the bedside chair, stretching out his arms and rolling his shoulders.

"Compton's not a bad player, you know, although I'll feel it tomorrow, I fear... especially this wrist."

"Oh, Bim, you really ought to take a long soak in the bath before evensong."

Bim finished stretching and looked fondly at his wife. She looked so neat sitting on the edge of the bed like that, her stockinged feet pulled beside her as she popped her earrings into a small box from her handbag.

"Baths are for ladies, my dearest. A shower will do fine."

"Anyway, you've diverted my line of thought. Supposing Sheikh Mohamed Imran were to become very ill or meet an untimely death, what safeguards would be put in place to ensure the Abbey protected the inhabitants?"

Bim paused by the ensuite door.

Visibly tensed, turning to his wife, he spoke in a low tone, "Darling, that is dangerous talk; you never know who may be listening. I think it pertinent to discuss such sensitive matters in our country residence."

He loosened his tie and undid the top buttons of his shirt, then continued in a louder, more jovial tone, "And don't forget, you promised the first dance at this evening's do."

Some time passed. Mrs Nkosi busied herself at the dressing table. She applied a fresh coat of lipstick and finished with a spritz of perfume. Mr Nkosi changed from the white to a pale blue shirt and began fastening the buttons.

"What time do we need to be there?"

"Evensong will be finished at around seven, so as long as I'm not accosted by that wittering brown-nosed junior minister again, we should be home by half past the hour, which allows us time to have an evening before drinks and nibbles begin."

"Oh, I think you're being unfair! Brown-nose, as you call him, is fresh out of university and trying his hardest to make a good impression."

"I have no interest in ministers who fly with the wind and hold no conviction in their assertions."

"Perhaps his youth allows him the freedom to change his opinions."

Bim took his wife by her slim shoulders.

"You fiery little thing, I hope you never change your opinion about me!"

Pauline wriggled playfully from his grasp. Once free, she strode towards the large sash window, which overlooked the Victorian courtyard. There were tables already set out for the evening's event, and staff were laying out glasses and napkins.

"Is there a proposed format for this evening's get-together? Which departments are coming?"

"The usual dear, transport, business, health, education... It's not a meeting but rather a bit of a thank-you to the team for cooperating under the immense pressure they've been under. It's been bloody relentless."

"So, just in-house, no special guests?"

"Ah..." Bim smiled and winced with the memory his wife was obviously referring to.

The Turkish Prime Minister's brother had taken rather a fancy to Pauline at the last party and received rather an earful from Bim's wife. While not altogether sorry for her sharp words, she wished she had known his position and dealt more tactfully with him so as not to create a long-lasting social awkwardness.

Chapter 9

Charlotte's eyes had puffed up considerably since her emotional explosion in the Stramford room. Taking herself to the small bathroom she shared with Pat, she soaked a face cloth in cold water, wrung it out and took it back into the room with her. Lying outstretched on the bed, she placed the cool cloth across her eyes. It felt nice.

Pat sat in the chair next to her bed, reading the stapled book they had received from Mother Pascal. Aside from occasional sighs or tuts, she remained mostly silent. She seemed engrossed as each revelation hit home. Finally breaking the silence, she spoke.

"Says 'ere that we cannot enter into any sort of sexual relationship with anyone on the premises. Who exactly are they referring to?! I wouldn't look twice at any of 'em!"

Pat meant it as a joke as her face looked expectantly at Charlotte, who was outstretched on the bed. Charlotte did not move, but her chest rose and fell slowly. Well, at least she isn't dead, Pat mused. May be a bad time to inform her companion that the next paragraph mentioned sterilisation where required. She rubbed the bridge of her nose and tried to remember the exact words of Mr Wilks. He had demanded that she appear very accepting of all the rules so as to lighten the blows to Charlotte. Pat didn't care much for how Charlotte took anything. It was clear she was a spoilt brat used to getting her own way and, as a result, would struggle to see further than her own misery. This didn't make for great company.

"'ow are you doin' Charlotte?"

No reply.

"Are you ready for Praise group?"

No reply.

"Not too sure why yer sulking with me m'love. Probably best to lick your wounds and crack on."

Pat stood up from the wooden chair and straightened the blanket covering her bed. Putting the book down on the chair she had just vacated, she stretched.

"We're expected in the Praise room in 'alf hour. You'll 'ave to be in a better state than that, or they'll chuck you in the med room."

"Oh, just fuck off, Pat!" Charlotte retorted.

"No need for language like that, young lady."

"It's alright for you to have all your goddamn liberties taken away, you've had your life already. You've probably got kids already, have you? You've probably had a job and a house and a nice garden... and a car! Oh, I miss my car!" fresh tears welled in Charlotte's eyes again, "Oh, this is hell. HELL!"

She kicked a sandal across the floor, hurting her toe in the process. Pat looked on in disbelief.

"Ain't you got any self-control, love? They won't tolerate that 'ere."

"Tolerate?! I'm not asking to be tolerated. I just want my old life back."

"From the sounds of things, your old life was funded entirely by yer dad."

"That's none of your business!"

"Well, it ain't sustainable, is it love? What about when yer dad gets old? Will he 'ave to provide for ye then? Yer right. It's none of my business, and I don't care much anyway, but quit your self-centred sobbing. It's very bloody distracting."

Charlotte glowered at the older lady and hobbled over to retrieve her sandal.

Once in the Praise room, Charlotte felt rather foolish. As she looked about the inhabitants of the group, she felt more and more humiliated. While these people were so ruined and broken, they still managed to keep some attempt at dignity, far from her embarrassing earlier explosion. One lady, horribly disfigured by burns, used her one good hand to knead a lump of clay. Her other hand was all but gone save one remaining finger, which she used to hollow out the dough into a bowl shape. Wandering over to her, Charlotte sat. She didn't know what to say, so she remained silent.

"Hello?" a pleasant voice surprised Charlotte as the burnt lady turned towards her.

"Are you the new lady? I was told you were starting today."

"Er... yes. I'm Charlotte, nice to meet you."

"You sound surprised! Did you expect me to howl like a wolf or something?!"

The lipless face showed teeth, though one side of the mouth was turned down.

"Don't be put off by how I look. You don't have to live with it each day; only I do that."

The teeth stayed prominent.

Charlotte didn't know where to look. There was hair on one side of the lady's face, a mousy blonde colour, and only one of her eyes seemed to focus. The other eye was closed shut, and the nose had melted away entirely. The skin changed from a thin, shiny red to heavily thick yellow scarring.

"I'm Tilly, by the way."

Charlotte felt a strong compulsion to run away. She wanted to bolt out the door and never look back, but at the same time, the voice compelled her to listen.

"You know people usually take one look at me and react in one of two ways."

She splatted the clay pot in the centre of her board and wiped her hand on a rag.

"Either they go super nice and chat incessantly to me without actually looking at me, or," she paused, looking round and straight into the face of Charlotte, "or they go all sad and regretful and try and offer suggestions as to how I can cope, through prayer or meditation, or therapies or even plastic bloody surgery... So which one are you?"

Charlotte sighed.

"Oh, God knows. I'm a spoiled brat, mostly self-centred, and generally a waste of space. How does that work?"

Tilly laughed, though most of her face did not change.

"I only heard this very morning that I'm stuck in this place apparently forever, and I'm not very bloody happy about it. I had something of a life out there, and now here I am in this gorgeous red polo shirt talking to you."

Tilly chuckled but, in a low warning voice, said, "Keep your voice down a bit, Charlotte, or they'll move you to someone else."

"I honestly don't care. I'm past caring."

"I'm guessing that's because they haven't punished you for anything yet. I remember others like you. They were full of life, dead funny, some of them! Then, over time, they were knocked about for insubordination, and they got progressively quieter and duller.

Charlotte looked straight at the horribly burnt woman.

"How old are you?" she asked.

"Try and guess."

"I think you're pretty young, say early twenties?"

"Wrong!"

"Sixty bloody four!"

The two ladies burst out laughing. A few red shirts looked their way, then turned back to whatever they were doing. Pat was over by the wizened Michael, adjusting his headphones and scrolling through a list of TV programmes.

"Yeah, well, no offence, but you look a bit of a bloody mess yourself," said Tilly.

"Yeah, maybe," Charlotte looked sad but then, with a wicked glint in her eye, said, "Says you?!"

Tilly's half-face broke into a smile again, "You're dead funny, you!"

"Oh, shut up! I've just discovered that I've no hope of ever escaping this awful place. I'm supposed to cleanse my soul before God or something for being so damn selfish all the time. I'm sure there's worse than me out there. I don't know why I had to be grabbed."

"You've probably got a rich uncle or something. Money pays for rich people's problems. Face it, you and me are problems."

Chapter 10

The young policeman had a thermal vest under his shirt; it warmed him but made his belt feel uncomfortably tight. He would like to have loosened it by a notch but would have to wait another hour or so. The wooden speech stand stood alone on the forecourt from the Chancellor's earlier announcement. He began to wonder whether clearing it away was in his job description. If he were to take it, where should he put it? Should he pop it in the door as he had the flying cat?

His thoughts were disturbed by a number of smart but plain-clothed officers who walked purposefully from the gates towards him. They were in discussion as they approached, and one taller man motioned at the speech stand and clicked his fingers impatiently. Without hesitation, the young officer walked over to pick up the stand and, not without difficulty, manoeuvred it to the front door. He knocked, and at once, his colleague from within the threshold took it.

By the time he took his position by the door again, there was a sleek black car purring up to the gates. The policeman had to keep his head facing forward and could not determine much from his peripheral vision, but could see that a number of gentlemen of possible Saudi descent were approaching. One particular man in a traditional dress could only have been royalty. The young officer bowed lightly and let the small party in.

Prime Minister's Questions had not gone particularly well for Bim. Famed for keeping remarkably cool under duress, Bim could feel the pressure building behind his temples and his veins throbbed uncomfortably as yet again the same photographs were brought up. Again and again, the Prime Minister had rebuffed claims with a cool smile and recommended that the opposition await the results of the report.

"Prime minister, do you or do you not deny that as leader of the great people of this country, you must be trustworthy first and foremost? If your own wife cannot rely on you to keep your pants on, how will the country be expected to believe in your honesty and integrity?"

The opposition fell about laughing and cheering. The Prime minister's chief advisor raised his hands at the speaker incredulously.

"Order! Order! Orderrrrrrrrrrr!"

Bim had found some comfort in his chancellor, John Singh, who was calm and astute and had remained loyal to him throughout even the earliest tumultuous days of the election. Right-wing, ill-disguised racism had created aggressive riots on the streets, the main theme being that the African giant was a godless ape who had bounded out of a primitive African jungle ready to impregnate every pure English woman he could get within his clutches. It was so bad it was almost laughable had it not been for the sinister trolling that continued to climb to unprecedented levels. It did seem that common sense prevailed, however, as the British public, against all the odds, made the polls fall in his favour.

The Prime Minister's head ached. He felt feverish and wondered if he was coming down with something. All was quiet now. His office telephone flashed its little red light calmly, matching the pulse he could feel throbbing in his neck. He put his head in his hands and shut his eyes a little while listening to the hum of the laptop and some distant shouting outside. A vehicle sounded its horn aggressively. Though its distance from Bim soothed him, he didn't mind ferocious lions in faraway cages. The phone chimed quietly but intrusively enough to disturb Bim's peace. With a sigh, he picked up the receiver.

"They have arrived, sir, and are taking light refreshments in the bar."

"Thank you. How long do I have?"

"Twenty minutes or so, sir, this side of 6 o'clock."

"Thank you, Teresa."

Bim replaced the handset. Was twenty minutes enough time to ring Pauline to see what she had made of the photographs, or would a text suffice? What the heck could he write in a text? He proceeded to type and then delete about four separate attempts at opposition political spin against him, then sighed and gave up. It would be better to discuss it in the privacy of their countryside home, and with any luck, Pauline would be arriving there within the next hour or so. He gave his watch a final glance, ran his hands over his hair and pulled his cufflinks straight.

Sheikh Mohamed Imran was sullen and uncommunicative. His translator, a young, wide-eyed man in a sharp suit, did all he could to coax something out of him, but it seemed the greatly revered Sheikh had not travelled particularly well and required further refreshment before talking business. His neatly trimmed beard was mostly black with greying sideburns and a scattering of white flecks under his chin. He was a little overweight, but he stood tall.

When Bim arrived, a visible change took over the Sheikh, and he sat straighter in his chair. His small entourage visibly relaxed at his change of countenance.

"Ah, the good Prime Minister joins us, Insha'Allah," Bim embraced the Sheikh with a warm handshake.

"It is good to see you again, dear Sheikh Mohamed Imran. It has been too long!"

The two gentlemen seemed to share a strong affinity for one another, which broke easily through the language barrier. The Prime Minister took the Sheikh by the arm and motioned that they sit beside the fire, which crackled enticingly.

"It is one of the finer British pastimes to sit by a roaring fire," Bim began.

The small translator instantly spoke the words to the Sheikh, who smiled courteously and spoke back in Arabic, looking intensely at Bim. A conversation ensued between the Sheikh and the Prime minister with the attentive, wide-eyed go between maintaining a steady stream of fluent Arabic and English. An agreement was made, and the entourage was shushed away by the Sheikh. Teresa, the Prime Minister's personal assistant, wore a tasteful head covering and ushered the guests into the formal meeting room, where they were offered refreshments and light entertainment. The young translator moved as if to go with them, but with a rough cuff round the ear by the Sheikh, he was brought back to the two men by the fireside.

"The young, huh? They know not what is good for them, huh?"

He smiled and proceeded to rub the hair of the young man in an exaggerated display of affection. He then spoke slow, malicious words in Arabic, to which the man bowed reverently and resumed his former place between the dignitaries.

"Now... how you saying... the rabble disperse... you have a stronger drink for an old man, huh?" the Sheikh smiled warmly at the Prime Minister.

Instead of looking in any way perturbed by the Sheikh's strange behaviour towards the translator, the Prime Minister smiled and, with a twinkle in his eye, gestured to a drinks cabinet in the corner of the elegant room.

"You don't mind, Sheikh Mohamed Imran, if I open something a bit special?"

"No, I mind not and for respect, I can offer to join you, Mr Prime Minister."

He held the large brandy glass and took a savoured sip.

"As you are knowing. My daughter Latifa (may Allah keep her safe) lies dying in the Abbey, the institution you, I believe, are aware of through your son, who is a resident too. I am right, Prime Minister, am I not?"

"Of course, and I am sorry for your sadness."

"It is an unbearable sadness, Prime Minister, because Latifa was not born this way. She was so very beautiful. Her eyes were shining like her mother's. I think she was not of this world, sir. She was a gift from God."

The Sheikh's eyes lost focus as he stared into the fire. He took a long sip of his brandy.

"You know her accident?"

Without warning, he slipped into a sad Arabic monologue to nobody in particular, though the translator perked up and listened hard.

"He says sad words for his daughter, Prime Minister. He misses her most keenly as she was the only child born of his most precious wife, Princess Fatima, who died in childbirth. He says she looked just like her mother, Prime Minister, her eyes were particularly beautiful, sir, she was a gift from Allah, he says this many times, and his heart is heavy, Prime Minister."

"But the accident? I think this was a riding accident?" Bim leaned towards the Sheikh, but it was the translator that answered.

"Yes sir, yes, it was reported in the media that the young princess was crushed to death by her horse. Though it was an untimely stroke that maimed her, it was a shock, Prime Minister, because she was so young. The best medics in the world tried to help her recuperate, but she was not the same."

"Not the same? My precious angel was killed and left a (how you say) half face? She twists one side up and one down, and it is not my daughter, I say. It is a monster. It is only Stramford, Mr Edward Stramford, who, how you say, founding, did founding the Abbey, and he was a most charming man, Mr Prime Minister."

"*Founded* Sheikh Mohamed Imran, Mr Stramford *founded* the Abbey," chipped in the translator.

"Ah! He corrects me; he is too much!" the Sheikh cuffed the young translator, making his dark hair fly across his forehead.

"The Mr Stramford took me to the King's Head. You know this bar, Prime Minister? We drink strong drinks, and he tell me all is not lost. He says I must not despair because he is founding the Abbey."

"Yes, Sheikh Mohamed Imran, there is no doubt it is a sanctuary for our most vulnerable," agreed the Prime Minister.

The Sheikh began a long speech, pausing only briefly to allow the translator to summarise and convey the Sheikh's intentions over to the Prime Minister.

"Sheikh Mohamed Imran is to invest, sir; he wants to buy the Abbey from Mr Stramford in its entirety. It is expensive, sir, but this is of no concern to the Sheikh, sir. It is the conditions of sale that rile him, sir. Mr Stramford has insisted that the institution is free from one particular religion and instead encompasses the spiritual needs of all its residents, including those of no religion at all. The term particularly upsets Sheikh Mohamed Imran, who insists that for the institution to be pure in its delivery of God's work, it will need to take on Islamic rule with sympathy towards other religions. This term is currently under review by both Sheikh Mohamed Imran's lawyer and those of Mr Stramford."

"Can I offer you a top-up, Sheikh Mohamed Imran?" Bim asked, offering the bottle toward the empty glass.

With an affirmative nod, Bim filled both glasses generously and spoke, "I think it is a commendable investment with much return, both financially and spiritually. I would suggest that many of the residents are likely from a spectrum of religious backgrounds and cultures; therefore, narrowing it to one overriding religion may turn away some of your most profitable partners. Perhaps you could draw up a new set of conditions agreed upon by both parties, which offer facilities catering to all spiritual as well as recreational requirements?"

The translator quickly conveyed the Prime Minister's thoughts, and the Sheikh nodded impatiently.

"You, Prime Minister, sir, I think you are understanding the importance of the Abbey. Your son make you to see how it can give peace to you. How you know, he be happy, they are pain-free, husbands, fathers..."

The Sheikh slipped back into Arabic.

"Sheikh Mohamed Imran wishes for you to be involved more directly in this business plan, using the British police and security to ensure a strict, smooth system within the Abbey. This allows a safe and well-ordered institution that will champion the best facilities and staff benefitting from outstanding training. He intends to extend beyond the small number of existing partners to allow more foreign investment. This will enable the Abbey to grow, allowing all business people over a certain wealth category to use the Abbey facilities to their advantage. The more investment it receives, the more the facilities can be used on a global stage. Sporting events can be staged on the grounds and broadcast all over the world, but the security will be first-class, ensuring everything on display is world-class. The Sheikh wishes to do this in honour of his late wife, Fatima."

Bim nodded thoughtfully, studying the Sheikh sitting opposite. He was obviously intelligent and had huge wealth behind him, some of which it seemed he was prepared to send in his direction. It sounded like a bold plan. Though there was no doubt it was achievable, he took his mind back to the tour of the Abbey he and Pauline took just last week. It really was a sanctuary, an immaculate gentleman's club with wonderful facilities and cheerful staff. Surely, anyone who was anyone would want to use their facilities or cast off any irritating family members to prosper there happily.

As the two powerful men slipped into a deeper, relaxed state of drunken stupor, save a few cuffs about the head, the translator felt that things had gone rather well. He hoped both were tired enough not to notice him slip away. Teresa arrived with three able-bodied staff members to carefully lift the Prime Minister out of his slumber and guide him upstairs to his private quarters to sleep it off.

The Sheikh's entourage similarly and with expert precision took their master back to the black car and swiftly placed him in the penthouse at the Ritz Hotel.

Pat held on to the hand of the dying young woman whose chest rose and fell with laboured breathing. Nodding to Jasmine, beautiful Arabic music descended into the room. The lady smiled, but her eyes remained closed.

"Latifa love, let me know if you feel comfy."

Pat leant close to the patient as if to hear her faintest whispers, but no sound came as the patient's face relaxed from the smile to a completely relaxed state, the mouth fell ajar, and the breathing became shallower. Each inhalation wheezed, and the exhalations rattled slightly. Pat gently massaged the patient's hands and lower arms, and Jasmine gently wiped her brow with a cool cloth. The emotional music echoed off the walls. A gentle breeze came in from the open window, and a bird song joined the crying sitar.

All was peaceful. Jasmine's lips moved in prayer, and Pat gently administered a dose of morphine.

Mother Pascal arrived to read the last rites and offered a short prayer for the life of Latifa Mohamed Imran. A drip was carefully changed, and the patient's eyes flickered open before her heart stopped. Mother Pascal reached forward to gently close the eyes of the young Asian woman.

The three women worked efficiently to clean the body and prepare it for the next instruction. Unusually, the funeral plans remained ambiguous, and the sisters did not know whether Sheikh Mohamed Imran wished to see the body of his daughter at all.

Chapter 11

Bim woke with a dull headache. His neck was at a peculiar angle as he began to come to, he stretched his head slowly to each side before lifting it from the pillow. As his gaze began to focus, he became aware of a presence in the room. Pauline's side of the bed was empty and he immediately remembered that she was in their countryside home. So, who was here? Feeling uncomfortable now, he pulled his legs round to the side of the bed and saw his clothes neatly folded on the chair.

"Hello?" He called out, pulling on his shirt. From the ensuite, he heard the toilet flush and the sink plug was released, making a glugging sound. Now completely dressed, save the tie, Bim stood staring at the closed ensuite door. It opened. Out walked the translator dressed in the same shirt and trousers he had been wearing yesterday evening.

"Just what the bloody hell do you think you're doing in my room?!" Bim spluttered in disbelief.

"Oh, I'm sorry, Mr Prime Minister, I was lost, I think, I am not able to find my group and I think you were now shut for the evening, so I have been resting on the sofa out there until I can join the group. I'm afraid my phone has no charge, so..."

"Get the hell downstairs and out of my sight, good God!" Bim rang the bell by his bedside desk and Teresa answered immediately.

"Morning, sir. Is everything ok?"

"Not really, Teresa. It seems that Sheikh Mohamed Imran's translator has found his way to my ensuite."

"Gracious! Please send him to me and I'll ensure he's taken back to his party."

Bim ushered him out of the door and shuddered at the potential headlines that could begin cascading all over the media. PM's pants down again, PM's sexuality in disrepute. A wave of nausea swept through him as he reached for his iPhone and the plans for the day.

Mother Pascal stepped smartly from the black cab and walked to the entrance of the large black and white country house. Ordinarily, she would have paused to admire the wildflowers carefully managed so as to look random yet sweeping the eye to the expanse of the garden beyond. Today, however, she was on an emergency call.

Before Mother Pascal even reached the brass knocker, the door opened and there stood Lady Pauline Nkosi, neat yet evidently in some distress.

"Oh Heather, you are so kind to come out like this. I just couldn't face the city and the press and... quite frankly, anything."

"I am here whenever you need me, Pauline. You look tired, dear. Have you had anything to drink?"

Pauline led Mother Pascal through to the large kitchen, there were cups and plates piled on surfaces and the bin stood overflowing in the corner. Deftly as if it were her own kitchen, Heather Pascal swept the dishes to the side and reached for the kettle.

"Are you alone, dear?" She filled it and popped it on the hob, moving straight to the cabinets to find teacups.

"Quite alone Heather," Pauline sighed, sitting herself on a kitchen stool and half twirling it. "I just needed a friendly face; there's been so much scrutiny of late like every person is so interested in my every damn move, it's exhausting."

"Yes dear, I saw the latest press coverage. "Do you know much about it? Are you ok?" She moved to the large refrigerator and stood studying the contents for some time before finding the milk.

"Oh, it popped up on my news feed at breakfast. It's not unexpected. We were ready for this sort of scandal... it's just, it's just that today felt different."

She brought her hand up to one of her earrings and twisted it gently.

"I'm plagued with guilt for Michael, which I know is utterly irrational, but I'm mixing Michael's needs as my son with my own needs to be a good mother. I cannot fulfil his needs here at home, I know he's happy with you. I just... I just need you to tell me that again so I know it's the truth rather than my own wishful thinking."

Heather Pascal handed a steaming cup of tea to the shaking woman and took a stool.

"Would you like a biscuit, my dear, or shall I get some scones delivered?"

"No, no, the tea is fine."

"As I said previously, Mrs Nkosi, I believe that you have done the honourable thing by releasing your son to spread his wings in the safety of the Abbey. This selfless act has allowed both you and Mr Nkosi complete freedom to work together to tackle one of the most intensive jobs in history. I believe Mr Nkosi is stronger with you, and indeed you with him. I understand, however, that since the birth of your son, it is highly natural that you will, as you so accurately describe, have yearnings to mother him or at least mourn what he might have become."

"That's it! That's it, Heather. What he might have become. I cannot mourn the loss of a son who lives still. I'm in a cruel limbo where all around me, I see other parents saturated with joy at their children's successes and I have to scrabble about with my job satisfaction as some kind of flat alternative. It's rotten, just rotten."

"It is God's way, Mrs Nkosi. I cannot pretend to understand the reasons. However, I can say with my whole heart that you have become a stronger, more spiritual person as a result, and it is through your experiences that you can relate so well to many of the population who are forgotten in a soulless system. I truly believe that you and your husband are pioneers in care for those unfortunate, such as your son."

"You paint me like some sort of heroine. I'm no such thing Heather, I'm a bloody fraud. I cannot even look after my son. How am I supposed to support the man who runs the whole country?"

"You're tired, my dear. I think you have not slept enough. It is your own troubled heart that is both your saviour and downfall. Please say prayers or look to the psalms with me."

The two women retreated to the lounge, took up their Bibles and read a number of much loved and well-known psalms to the more elusive little-known ones. Discussing them at length meant that Pauline felt a great weight lifting from her shoulders as she entered into a more open state of mind, free of worldly problems and full of love for her faith.

"I think Heather, that I feel much better now. I am so grateful that you came out here for me. I can only describe what I felt as a sort of suffocation of my soul."

"My dear, you are not the first and most definitely will not be the last great woman to seek strength from the Bible."

A key turned in the lock and the door clicked open.

"Hello, love!"

Pauline leapt up and walked to the hall to greet her husband.

"I'm so glad you're home, darling. I expected you later."

The Prime Minister gave a nod and a wave to his driver, who retreated to the car. He pulled his briefcase into the hall and began to unbutton his overcoat.

"Ah, Heather, lovely to see you. I trust you are well?" He nodded politely to Mother Pascal, who had emerged from behind his wife.

"Good evening, Prime Minister. I am quite well, thank you. I will not encroach any further on your time. I know how time is precious!"

"Don't rush off on my account, please. How is Michael faring? I was going to make a call this evening, but you can let me know first-hand."

"Michael is quite well, Mr Nkosi. He is responding very well to his pain control medication, though it can make him rather sleepy on occasion. He knows he can go to his private bedroom at any time if he feels lethargic, and the staff will ensure that he receives a full timetable of activities around his naps."

"Good, good." Bim smiled politely, then made excuses to head to his office for a short while.

"Would you like a coffee love?" Pauline called after him, but he appeared not to hear.

A short while later, Mother Pascal made her way out of the grand country house, driving along narrowing country roads until finally she met the dual carriageway and fast tracked towards the Abbey. She thought hard about Pauline and concluded that if the world was populated with thoughtful and selfless people like her, it would be a much kinder place to exist.

Once Mother Pascal was safely out of the house, Bim returned to the kitchen wearing his slippers and holding their ginger tabby under his arm.

"Everything ok, my dear? I assume you've seen the latest scandal? It's infantile, it really is and I'm absolutely done with Langstone and his party of clowns."

He gently placed the cat on the windowsill, pulled his tie off and threw it unceremoniously on the kitchen side.

"It's a bit messy here, darling. Have you been entertaining?"

"No Bim, I haven't, I'm afraid this is all my own filth. I was having a bit of a down couple of days and couldn't muster the strength to wash a single dish. It's pretty appalling and I'm going to do the lot myself now that I'm feeling better."

Pauline skipped lightly over to her husband and began to massage his shoulders.

"I feel much better now you're home."

"Likewise, my dear. Did you make that coffee, by the way? I could do with it. You would not believe my last few days."

Pauline moved over to the coffee machine that flashed a 'service me' warning light on the screen. "Darling, I'm not sure this will actually produce coffee in its current state.

Bim clicked his tongue in annoyance.

"Damn this technology, use the old cafetiere or something."

"Fine, it's been a while since we shared one of these anyway." Pauline mused while filling the kettle.

"Tell me about your last few days. You were meeting the Sheikh, weren't you? What did he want?"

"He is buying the Abbey Pauline. He's buying the whole institution from Stramford and it looks set to happen soon. The solicitors are sorting the finer details, but it appears that save a few unbreakable clauses, the Sheikh is free to run it as he pleases."

Pauline looked horror stricken and Bim raised his eyebrows in surprise.

"You look shocked, darling. Why? It's no surprise that a profitable enterprise of any sort should attract the attention of these mighty Sheikhs."

"But he is notoriously ruthless! He's not going to run that place for the good of the residents. It'll be run entirely for profit, surely? I'm assuming he'll want to expand? Oh, imagine. This is just what I feared from the outset. The Abbey, as it stands now, is based on trust and love. I wholeheartedly believe that the happiness of the inhabitants is based on a shared belief in its system, that of ensuring that our most vulnerable in society have the right to live out enriching lives that come to an end naturally and with dignity... I fear that the Sheikh will lose focus on what the Abbey is about and run it purely as a rich man's jail. Imagine who would end up within its walls?"

"Oh, my dear, I think you exaggerate. There's no harm in expanding the Abbey. He put forward a good business proposition, offering top-class facilities that could be used on the world stage for sporting events and more. The security would be stepped up, but not to its detriment. Rather the whole place would be superbly managed with landscaped gardens and immense sporting facilities. I cannot predict what, as it would depend on external investment."

Bim walked over to the kitchen sink window and looked out to the gardens.

"Any investors could be taken on potentially, the sciences, the arts, cutting edge medical care…. The Abbey would boast top security."

"But how Bim? How would any security team operate such an establishment without resorting to the Sheikh's favourite system of… of brutality?"

"Because, my love, it is my police team that will be operating under the Sheikh, that is why he came and spoke to me directly. The British police force stands alone as the most effective in the world and it is because of this, Sheikh Mohamed Imran wants to utilise this as he embarks on his business venture. He may seem bullish to you, but I can assure you he is not inhuman. He is as driven by his faith as you and it is not in anyone's interest to break an institution that has proven itself to be a success for over a decade now."

Pauline filled the cafetiere to the line and placed the gold plunger carefully on top. The lightness she had felt only moments before was leaving her and being replaced with a gnarled hand of doubt gripping her about the throat. She tried to swallow it down and handed her husband his coffee.

"Here, love."

Chapter 12

The alarm sounded and Charlotte's eyes flickered open. The room was awash with morning sunshine and the sound of birds chittering so near that Charlotte wondered if they were actually in the cabin. Pale grey cigarette smoke wafted away from the open window where Pat was sitting and back into the room, settling lightly on the bedding and carpet.

"Morning Pat"

"Mornin' love."

"You're up early. Couldn't sleep?"

"I'm alright love, just lost in thought y'know."

Charlotte stretched and made a wobbly, stiff walk to the bathroom.

"Anything I can help with, Pat?"

"You're alright love, just crack on."

Charlotte splashed cool water on her face and dabbed it dry with the towel. She took a long, hard stare at herself in the mirror. Save the puffy morning eyes, she looked ok, better than she used to anyway. Remembering her pre-Abbey days, staring in the mirror had been rather frightening at times. She'd often woken up terribly hungover and dehydrated. Black makeup streamed down her cheeks and then dried in mucky patches cast by her sleeve. She hadn't looked after herself at all as a young adult, eating poorly, drinking far too much and sleeping off and on between parties. This new Charlotte looked nice, she had colour about her cheeks and a sparkle in her eyes. She took up a hairbrush and began to run it through her hair. It looked sleek and glossy. She thought about pictures of her mother pre-cancer, she too, had looked this way. It gave Charlotte a dull pain in her gut to think about it.

"It's Sunday, love. We've got prayers in 'alf an hour."

Charlotte sat on the edge of her bed and studied Pat, still smoking by the window.

"Why do we all have to go to the church if we're not religious whatsoever? It seems daft to me. I'd be more use mucking out the stables."

Pat looked tired and let out a sigh.

"It's the way the Abbey enforces their ethos to all the staff, through the word o' God. Without guidance from the church, all the staff would be outta control, hell bent on fulfilling their own desires, which very rarely involve giving much of a damn for anybody else. Whatever your religious views are, love, you could do wi' learning a bit about humility and selflessness."

"You're no angel Pat, even I can see that. Why would you resign yourself to following the system here if you don't believe in it?"

"It may surprise you to hear this love, but I do believe in it. When it works, it works well an' even navel gazers like you can be a part of summat wonderful... It's about love Charlotte, it's about people takin' care of each other, it's about tolerance for each other. It's about giving summat back."

Charlotte flopped back on the bed.

"So it's the idea you like, right? You like the idea of spoilt rich kids giving something back to the community by means of helping more vulnerable rich kids in society?"

"It ain't as simple as that. You're just lookin' from your perspective. There's people 'ere from all over the world, talented people in different fields, they use the Abbey as a safe space to explore their ideas and stuff, I don't really get it love. All I know is that we're in somethin' big right 'ere. It's bigger than you, it's bigger than me and if you keep yer 'ead down and behave yerself, then you'll be a bigger part of it."

"A part of what?! You're talking in code, for God's sake Pat. A part of what? A bloody care system for the rich that doesn't sound too groundbreaking to me."

"Yer just a tiny cog 'ere Charlotte. You're just 'elping out the Praise group unless you prove yourself to be useful in other ways. Remember Charlotte, this place ain't about you pleasin' yourself, it's about what you can do to 'elp the Abbey as a whole."

115

Charlotte put on her red polo shirt and wriggled on the jeans. Pausing for a moment, she looked back over to Pat.

"I honestly don't think you came here when I did. I'm sure you've been here way longer than me."

Pat looked straight into the eyes of her roommate and took a long and final drag on her cigarette before carefully extinguishing it on a large stone placed for that purpose on the window ledge. With an audible sigh, Pat came over to Charlotte and sat beside her on the bed.

"You are wading about in treacherous waters, love, any waves from you and it ain't just your 'ead on the line, it's mine. Do you understand? You're my little soddin' responsibility. I need to know that if I talk open to you, you ain't gonna drop me in it. I swear you'll be killed outright or messed up so much you'll be a new addition to the Praise group. Are you followin' me? I've seen it all 'appen before. You cannot stick your independent little neck out in this place or it'll be sliced clean off. Am I gettin' through to you?"

Pat was so close that Charlotte could feel her trembling slightly. The cigarette breath of the woman hung in the air, mixed with fear and conspiracy.

"Am I actually in danger, Pat?"

"No, you ain't if you do what you're told! If you continue to help them poor souls in praise group and undertake whatever work you're set diligently enough, you'll be fine,

116

you WILL be fine, but I'm tellin' you straight love, coz I can see the feisty arsed piece of work that you are, that if you're planning some magnificent escape or summat, pack it in now."

"So all that crap about this place being... practically ethereal was just to make me conform, right?"

"No, you bloody idiot. This place was set up as a pioneering venture by one of the kindest hearted men I ever 'eard ."

"You knew him?"

"He was a well-known business tycoon, Stramford 'is name was. He made millions, but he was different to the others. He was compassionate and thoughtful, he was constantly tryin' to give back to 'is community. He set up schools, children centres an' all that stuff, but it never quite worked, coz they weren't run by like-minded people. So, he decided to set up the Abbey, where he had complete control of how things were run. At the heart of the place were the teachings of Christianity. He was a devout Christian y'see."

"He would be..." Charlotte muttered with an eye roll.

"With an attitude like yours..." Pat growled, standing upright suddenly and making her way out of the door for morning prayers.

Charlotte regretted her eye roll. It wouldn't help to make an enemy of Pat. The empty cabin hummed quietly from one of the electric points by the chest of drawers. The silence was a new experience for Charlotte. In her old life, there was no such thing. The telly blared, or playlists blasted out of the Alexas. If no devices were on, Charlotte's trusty phone was always there. She could scroll through social media for hours on end, usually half drunk or half asleep.

The silence opened possibilities. It allowed Charlotte to step into thoughts and really focus on them from birth to conclusion. It allowed her to properly listen to the sounds of insects, birds or changing weather. She could hear the click of the thermostat and the sighing of the floorboards as they creaked post footstep. She lay back on the bed. She knew it was prayer time. Pat had just left and she would hurry not to be late. Charlotte felt strangely calm. It was as if nothing mattered anymore. Maybe she would just have a small doze, no one would miss her at prayers, would they...? Admittedly, she had never missed a session yet. The expressions on both Jasmine and Bernadine's faces when Charlotte had even joked about such a thing had been so bleak that she had not pushed her luck. But perhaps today, she would. Pat had effectively told her to behave or be killed, which, although Charlotte had no doubt was loaded with genuine fear, seemed so mediaeval in theme that she supposed it would result in little more than a sharp word from one of the suits or a slap from Mother Pascal. A devilish curiosity in Charlotte rose somewhere about her midriff. What would actually happen if she didn't conform? How satisfying it would be to yell some home truths to that tight-faced Mother Pascal, giddy with her own magnificence. Risky, though it seemed, a good verbal duel held strong appeal...

After prayers, there would be choir. After choir would be the Praise group. After the Praise group, there would be kitchen help, then lunch and then recreation time. Charlotte could cuddle the horses if she liked. She could play tennis or wander down to the gardens, where she would find Pat, who loved and held great knowledge about the gardens. The open landscape stretched for miles, punctuated with different Abbey buildings, the squash courts, the science centre, the hospital block and the swimming pool. All off shot from the single most central building, the Abbey itself. She had not been in many of the buildings and had only discovered their function through questioning of red shirts that dotted the landscape. They made Charlotte think of the military, the way they all ran meaningfully to their duties, there was no back chat, leering or slouching. They were submissive yet cheery, especially the younger men. The women seemed more skittish. After a long and peaceful few moments stretched out on her bed, Charlotte finally decided that during recreation time, she might like to go to the library and choose one of the comfortable lounger chairs to curl up with a book.

The door burst open. It was Bernadine. She looked terrified.

"Charlotte! Why weren't you at prayers?"

"I... er... I lost track of the time."

"Oh Charlotte, you can't say that. You need to say you're ill, say you're ill or something."

Bernadine's pale hands were clasped together, something Charlotte noticed. She did a lot.

"Don't worry Bernadine. It's my problem, not yours."

"Charlotte get up, just get up. You have to come with me. We have to go to see Mother Pascal and Mr Wilks. Quick Charlotte, please."

"Okay, okay, I'm coming but Bernadine, calm yourself down!"

The young woman paced the room with such an anguished look upon her face that Charlotte began to feel guiltily responsible. She allowed herself to be taken by the hand and the two women broke into a run towards the Abbey. At the entrance, they took a sharp left down the corridor and fast walked towards the Stramford room.

"Are we not going to choir? Surely it's starting now?"

"No Charlotte, I have to leave you here. I think you will be done before the Praise group. They need you there." Bernadine lowered her voice and looked about her before whispering.

"Say you were ill Charlotte, please. You might get away with it because you're new."

They arrived at the door. Bernadine knocked and stood back. Charlotte stood firm, feeling invigorated by the run.

The door opened and Bernadine slipped away unseen. Charlotte immediately clocked the red shirted security guard with his concealed taser. She met his eyes coolly and with a confidence she didn't entirely feel.

"Sit."

Charlotte sat. She saw Mother Pascal, the Indian gentleman and Mr Wilks, who gazed intently back at her. A vivid deja vu made her feel slightly giddy. The hot tears pouring down her cheeks seemed babyish and embarrassing, yet she felt their wetness on her cheeks and how they stung her eyelashes and dripped splots on her red shirt. She forced her brain away and back to the immediate. An empty chair stood at the circular table.

"You did not arrive at prayers. Why?"

"I'm ill."

"You are not ill." Mr Wilks spoke slowly, separating each word.

"I am. I have a sore head. I felt weak and couldn't get up."

An adjoining door at the back of the room clicked open partially and a voice could be heard from within. Charlotte continued with confidence.

"I felt unwell and thought I had better stay in bed until I was fit to join everyone. Maybe I've picked up something. It wouldn't be right to pass on my bugs to..."

Charlotte stopped. Mr Wilks had raised his hand.

"No resident at the Abbey makes any sort of self-assessment about their health at any time. Your responsibility is to turn up punctually to all scheduled appointments and activities. There are procedures in place to ensure that every resident is in good health to partake fully in the daily running of this institution. I do not accept that you did not know this, as you were given a manual to familiarise yourself with weeks ago. Therefore, if you have decided to willingly boycott your duties here, you will have to accept the consequences of your actions."

Charlotte looked away from Mr Wilks to Mother Pascal as she felt sure a ghost of a smile flickered across her hardened face.

"What if I disagree with the policies outlined in your manual?"

"However you feel about anything bears no relevance to the Abbey. You are insignificant and become more so, the more you willingly dismiss the system. You may be familiar with self-destruction, which is evident in your case before you came here; however here at the Abbey, we believe in a unilateral mindset, so if indeed you had read the manual given to you, you would see that all the care staff in your section will have to undertake your punishment with you in equal measure." Mr Wilks placed both hands on the table and stood. Flattening down his tie with one hand, he walked over to where Charlotte sat.

"So you say you are ill?" He prompted in a quieter voice as he was near. "Yes," Charlotte felt horribly well.

Mr Wilks reached into his lapel pocket, causing Charlotte to jump in shock. She threw her arms up instinctively to protect herself, then instantly recognised the expected taser was, in fact, a thermometer. Feeling sheepish, she lowered her arms and cursed her jangly nerves.

Mr Wilks took her temperature and moved back to the table. He rejoined Mother Pascal, showing her the thermometer as he sat. Mother Pascal nodded and sat forward, locking Charlotte's gaze in her own.

"I will ask you again, Charlotte. Are you ill?"

"Yes"

"Well, I think you're looking the best I've ever seen you."

In walked the familiar bearded figure of Mr Compton. Charlotte choked.

"Dad?!"

Chapter 13

"Charlotte, it is good to see you."

Mr Compton pulled up the empty chair and sat, putting his elbows on the table and cupping his face with his hands. He studied her closely.

"I don't think I've ever seen you looking so well."

Charlotte was lost for words.

"I have watched you blossom from afar and it gives me great pleasure to see you develop into the kind and considerate girl I always knew you could be." He sat back in his chair and looked on fondly.

"I would never have thought that the change would be so... instantaneous."

"You're... you're looking at me like I'm a prize racehorse or something, Dad."

She felt tears brimming but blinked them angrily away.

"Why has it taken you this long to come and see me? How could you bring me here?!"

"You needed time to heal Charlotte. You were broken. It made you ugly."

"Ugly? Who's ugly?!" She spluttered an uncomfortable laugh and took a moment to recover.

"Alright, Dad, you've made your point. Let's go home."

"I don't mean physically ugly, I mean spiritually. You were becoming a selfish stranger, spiralling into a cycle of self-absorbed destruction. It was terrible to witness."

Mr Compton's brow furrowed with concern.

"I gave you everything Charlotte, everything you could possibly need... and more."

"Oh, I know... I know, Dad." Charlotte felt childish and pathetic. Prior to arriving at the Abbey, she hadn't given much thought to her actions; there was always a pressing physical need that overrode her conscience. The need for money, clothes, music, alcohol, parties, and dancing.

"Well, you can see things are going swimmingly well here too." She gave an apologetic smile.

Mr Compton suddenly stood up and with a nod to the two gentlemen and Mother Pascal, watched them take their leave. They left through the adjoining door at the back of the room. The Indian gentleman had a tablet computer, which he showed to Mr Compton as he passed.

"Friday late afternoon? You'll need to check that with Mr Nkosi. Send me a draft first."

The man nodded and tucked the small tablet into his shoulder bag.

"Heather, I'll need to see you for the medical reports." He said as she followed the two men.

Mother Pascal paused at the door.

"Of course, I've 2:30 scheduled if that's still acceptable?"

"Yes, of course, Heather, I'd actually forgotten!" He gave her a warm smile, which she returned, much to the surprise of Charlotte, who thought the woman had stopped just short of having a scaly tail and horns hidden within her clothes and hair.

The two were left alone in the Stramford room. Charlotte felt all her snarling anger ebb away. She felt entirely different from how she supposed she would feel alone with her father. Contrary to the whirling rage she had felt on learning that he was most likely responsible for her incarceration, she felt a calm realisation that pieced the mystery together. She was a brat, who ruined his peace. He gave her complete freedom to choose her path, but save for destroying herself altogether. She'd shown clearly that she could not cope. He had taken decisive action to bring her here in the hope of saving her from herself.

"You will have to behave here, Charlotte."

"I noticed."

"The Abbey is not lenient with a deliberate misdemeanour, and you must know that I cannot jump in and save you. It is written in law forbidding special allowances for any individual within the workforce."

"I'm in the workforce?"

"Yes, Charlotte, you are a carer."

"But why? Why on earth did you make me a carer, Dad? Why couldn't you have put me in the... I don't know, the science department or something?"

"Because selfishness is your biggest downfall, without seeing how your actions can help others, you will continue to isolate yourself and self-destruct. As your father, I'm not prepared to watch you do that again."

"But dad, I'll be tearing my hair out with boredom."

"As you have already seen, there are a multitude of activities you can entertain yourself with during recreation time. Just see and behave yourself so you have the freedom to enjoy them. Bernadine is waiting, you must go with her now."

Charlotte wondered how her father knew that Bernadine was outside as she watched him retreat to the adjoining door at the back of the room. The red shirt security man went to open the main door for her and sure enough, there stood Bernadine, fingers interlocked.

The praise group felt melancholy. The staff who usually smiled at Charlotte, seemed distant and sulky even. The Chinese lady with the beautiful plait looked away as Charlotte nodded a hello. One of the men who usually made coffee, didn't offer one to her. Only Tilly was as cheerful as ever and pleased to see her.

"What've you done Charlotte? I knew it wouldn't take you long to rock the boat."

Charlotte sat, wishing she had a coffee and turned to her half-melted companion.

"Oh, I was ill and couldn't attend prayers this morning... but they don't believe me, so apparently some terrible punishment is going to be dealt across the whole care team. The point of this is to attack my conscience and make me feel terribly guilty," Charlotte looked pointedly at the carers cradling their coffees.

"But do you know what Tilly? I don't even *have* a conscience, so it makes no difference to me anyway."

Tilly chortled though her terrible burns.

"Do you know what the punishment even is? It looks like no one's talking to me except you, and you won't know because the whole point of this place is to make life as pleasant for you as possible, right?"

"Yes, it sure is. So instead of wallowing in this god-awful atmosphere Charlotte, how about you put some music on or something?"

Charlotte sighed and made her way over to the Alexa. Two red shirts who were nearby scattered in different directions as if she had the plague. Turning to catch the eye of Tilly, Charlotte whispered to the device.

Suddenly, a great trumpet fanfare erupted all around the room. Charlotte leapt into a swirl and stopped abruptly as the trumpets ceased. The attention of the room caught. Without further ado, a rhythmic beat began bouncing off the walls, flamenco guitars burst through the device, Charlotte swept in a frenzy of movement, the swirls of the invisible frock cascaded around her. She kicked off her shoes and with greater freedom now, she circled the room, stamping her feet to the rhythm. Her hair loosened out of the tail and loose tendrils flew like streamers. Every face was transfixed, and the beauty of the dancewas that the woman who was a mere brat had transformed into something unworldly, making shapes and movements with her body that hypnotised every onlooker. The door clicked open and several people entered the room. They paused, entranced by the music, the swirling woman, and the moment.

Then it stopped. As quickly as it had all begun. It stopped.

A nervous clap ensued from one of the red shirted men, to be joined by the Chinese girl, and then they all erupted into rapturous applause with whoops of excitement, smiles beamed freely. Charlotte, flushed and joyous, leaned into an exaggerated curtsy again, then again, as her chest heaved from the exertion.

Bernadine had a huge smile across her face and Jasmine glowed with pleasure. Even Pat, one hand leaning on the table, looked openly impressed. It was only when Charlotte looked back at Bernadine that she noticed a tangible change in mood. The young woman's face had clouded over as she noticed the small party of people who had slipped unnoticed into the room. The clapping stopped abruptly and the red shirts immediately went back to their duties.

"Impressive." Mr Wilks spoke contemptuously.

"To what do we owe this brazen display of... exuberance?" He walked, slow clapping over to Charlotte, who still had to gasp slightly for breath.

"I must say it is strangely celebratory behaviour for one who is to spend the next three days in isolation."

Charlotte put her hand on a nearby chair for support, not just because she was tired, but in the same way, she'd curled her fingers around the fork in the stables. The height of the man as he looked down on her made her plummet back to earth, small and childlike. She clutched the chair harder. Tilly's voice suddenly cut through the tension.

"Mr Wilks, your time, if I may?" She made her way over, the burnt side of her crumpled slightly though her stump like arms moved with determination.

"I hope very much that the volume of the music did not disturb you, or indeed the content. I requested that Charlotte dance like that for me, as it is one of the pleasures I lost when my body was near destroyed in the terrible fire."

Mr Wilks looked nauseated by the figure. He nodded politely to her as she approached but took a step back as one might from a snake. Tilly continued.

"What makes Charlotte's act particularly thoughtful is that she felt so crushed by the news of her punishment prior to her dance. I felt she carried the world on her shoulders. I really do hope that you will be lenient with her, poor thing... though, of course, it is not my place to say."

"Miss Stephenson, I am sure Charlotte is most flattered by your concern. I will, of course consider your words carefully."

With that, he took a step back, turned on his heel and swept out of the room as if he couldn't get out of there quickly enough. The other suits lingered for a while as if to oversee that calm had returned, then they too, left the room to the palpable relief of the red shirts.

Coffee in hand, Charlotte soon learned of the punishment that was to befall the whole team. Contrary to her boastful earlier words to Tilly, she felt terribly guilty that the whole team of carers would have to forego their recreation time after work for a full three days and instead spend hours in the chapel reflecting upon their faith andconduct. Their knees would burn from endless kneeling. Their heads would ache from reading passage after passage from the Bible and they would sleep fractiously from lack of movement and fresh air they so craved during recreation time.

The one blessing Charlotte felt was that she did not have to see their faces as they suffered. She was taken away separately and put into a solitary cell with nothing but walls and a single pendant light fitting. The toilet was clean enough, though it had lost its seat, and she could just make out sounds of the outside world through a high up vent in the corner. On day one, she counted the bricks and created her own mini fitness routine. On day two, she did handstands against the wall and tried to conjure positive memories of her youth, though it was hard as so often unbidden ghosts reared up and sat heavy on her shoulders. On day three, she stayed motionless as if to slow the gnarled spectre of depression as it loomed closer.

Seated present were the Prime Minister, the foreign secretary and British government ministers for policing and security. Surrounded by a heavy security presence was Sheikh Mohamed Imran and three other family members. Mr Stramford, now very frail, was flanked by two high profile lawyers. The American president appeared via video link along with the Head of MI6. Laptops hummed in unison as the legal document was brought forth and signed by Mr Edward Stramford and Sheikh Mohamed Imran. The two gentlemen shook hands and posed for the momentous photo to certify the transaction had taken place legitimately and with the blessings of all major powers.

Chapter 14

At their countryside home, Bim woke with a spring in his step. He got the coffee going, fed the cat and enjoyed a delightful continental breakfast with Pauline. The morning sunshine poured through the kitchen window leaving the ledge warm for the pleasantly full cat to groom. The morning papers lay untouched on the breakfast table next to the marmalade, now empty toast rack and the cafetiere. Still with a post-shower towel on her head, Pauline scrolled through her Twitter account.

"Hooray! It appears Larry the Cat is receiving more media attention than you this morning."

"Oh really? What's he been up to now?"

"It seems he caught a raven of all things, and a reporter has declared it's one from the Tower of London!"

"Cats won't go for a raven, surely? It'd fight back.... and Larry?! Never!"

"It's coincidental, obviously, but his timing is brilliant! 'Springwatch' were beside themselves when one of the famous ravens disappeared two days ago. I think some of their eggs didn't hatch and some accidentally fell out of the nest, so Twitter folklore is unprecedented, they're saying it's an awful omen, the demise of the ravens."

Bim placed his empty coffee cup on the table and took his last bite of croissant. Dusting away the crumbs with his napkin, he checked his phone.

"I've got half an hour till I'm picked up. Are you sure you don't want to head over with me?"

Pauline threw the dregs of her coffee down the sink and swilled water around the cup.

"No, I'm going to clear up here a bit first. I'm going to meet the girls for high tea in the village and I'll head over late in the afternoon. You're in meetings most of the day, aren't you?"

"Yes, I'll need briefing for PMQs but after that, it's usual cabinet meetings and so on. I'll be at the Abbey briefly tomorrow."

Soon, Bim Nkosi was rolling back up to No. 10, briefcase in the back, head slightly fuzzy from the long drive coupled with the large Cognac the night before. The transport minister was first to arrive at his desk with a quick pre-meeting project summary. Teresa was sharper than usual, which showed she was under a lot of pressure. Bim, although concerned for his PA, could not allow himself to be distracted this morning. He had a long day to get through, with many meetings needing to run like clockwork.

Mid-afternoon, shortly after lunch, Teresa messaged the PM with an urgent call from Mr Sheikh Mohamed Imran, who insisted on speaking with him as a matter of urgency. Sighing at the now imminent cancellation of the quick pint he had hoped to grab downstairs, he took the call. Knowing the Prime minister very well, Teresa ran down to the bar and secured him an ice-cold real ale and salty peanuts to accompany. He smiled appreciatively at her and looked away, back into the middle distance...

"He's there now, surely?" Bim furrowed his brow in frustration.

"The chief of security, sir? Yes sir, he is here sir, but there seems to be a miscommunication. He is not understanding Mr Sheikh Mohamed Imran, sir," the translator babbled nervously.

"How is he not understanding him? You're a translator. Surely this is what you do?"

There was a minor kerfuffle at the end of the phone and then the distinct clear voice of Sheikh Mohamed Imran came down the line.

"Mr Prime Minister. I am needing you here with urgency. The man you are sending is... incompetent. He is refusing to do what I am requiring."

"I'm sorry, Sheikh Mohamed Imran. You've lost me. Is James there?

James Leighton?"

There were more background sounds as the phone moved against cloth, then into different hands.

"Mr Nkosi? Bim? Can you hear me ok?"

"Hi James, I can hear you fine. Is everything ok?"

"I'm afraid it's a no-go sir. I'm unable to impart any advice to the Sheikh and I genuinely fear the results of his intentions. I have my team here awaiting instructions and they're being shouted at like army recruits. Going along with this is bizarre and against my better judgement."

"Ok James, hold on in there. I'm going to head over in the next half hour or so."

He replaced the receiver, threw on his blazer and headed over to Teresa in her office. Fortunately, he caught her midway down the corridor.

"Sir, I've the education minister on the phone, he's requested a meeting as soon as possible."

"I'm sorry Teresa, you'll have to schedule him in tomorrow morning. I need to get over to the Abbey now. Is there a car outside?"

"Of course sir, I'll just phone down."

The Prime minister turned on his heel, went down the stairs and soon reached the doorman. He was greeted with a polite nod and guided to the waiting car. Once seated and watching the cityscape in motion, he called Teresa, requesting she find a translator who was both competent and unflappable.

She did. Hassan appeared within the hour. His arrival was deemed a success by Sheikh Mohamed Imran, who took great delight in firing his poor translator, sending him scurrying unceremoniously out the door. Hassan watched his miserable rival with professional indifference. He had been trained in the military and gave nothing away.

James visibly relaxed in Hassan's company as his presence offered a sense of order that had so lacked before. After introductions, James, the chief of security, highlighted his concerns through Hassan to the Sheikh and he, much calmer, now offered diplomatic solutions deemed acceptable by all parties. The chief concern from James was the manner in which the Sheikh directed his team which, in James' view, simply would not do. They needed clear guidelines as to the Sheikh's security vision so they could encompass that in their approach. They needed information on the use of drones, central locking systems, areas that needed to be physically manned and procedures in place for potential disarray. James's estimation of the Sheikh went up significantly once he stopped barking orders at them and he proved himself to be proactive rather than reactive in his methodology, which is what James had initially feared.

Once James and his team received a full briefing, there was a tangible excitement in the air. Many important guests were due to arrive on the premises in a matter of weeks and this gave the chief of security an excellent opportunity to showcase his team.

Sheikh Mohamed Imran liked his new translator very much and was grateful to Bim for providing him. It was the hardworking Teresa that had produced the goods, though Bim was happy to take the credit. James was much happier too, though he was clearly suspicious of the Sheikh and thought his spectacular dismissal of his former translator was wholly unacceptable.

An office was cleared next to the Stramford room and luxurious-looking furniture began arriving, expensive paintings, ornate tapestries and opulent curtains and drapes. The Abbey staff scurried about like ants, fetching and carrying. They had been gathered together and briefed prior to the Sheikh's arrival and told on no uncertain terms to keep out of his way or suffer his sandal up their arse.

Charlotte and Jasmine were partnered together in the kitchen preparing ingredients for the Sheikh's specific lunch requirements, much to the dismay of poor Mr Romano, who swore profusely and wrung his hands at the absolute cheek of the Sheikh demanding out of season obscure vegetables and complicated puddings he had barely heard about let alone made. His usual Italian outbursts saved for teasing the redshirts or bemoaning a cooking disaster now ran free and with gusto. Jasmine couldn't decipher the swearing from the anguished roars of Italian frustration, so both women chopped furiously and did their best to pacify him.

Finally, with two garnished plates of finest Ruz Al Bukhari, Romano looked fit to collapse.

"I'm not knowing if the rice is the right consistency for the Sheikh and if the fragrances are of the right strength, oh lord, I'm done for, old Romano is done for!"

He took a large swig of red wine and pulled his apron up and across his brow.

"I just cannot believe it."

Seven other plates were lined up, Jasmine held the garnishes ready, and Charlotte had the sauce ready to swirl artistically at the last minute.

Bernadine arrived dressed in her traditional habit, her hair tactfully covered for the Sheikh. She carefully picked up the two completed plates and swept them out of the kitchen to the dining room. The red shirt at the door opened it for Bernadine to enter and closed it carefully behind.

Seated was Mr Wilks, Sheikh Mohamed Imran, The Prime Minister and several more men Bernadine did not recognise. She knew she had to bring these particular dishes to both the Sheikh and the Prime Minister and then follow on with the others. She could see the door opening and more red shirts bringing plates for the other guests.

She nervously leant onto the table to put down the plates and was hit by the strong scent of cologne. Time seemed to slow as she took in the grandeur of the decorated table, fresh scented herbs and flowers, tall candles on sparkling brass holders, bejewelled napkin rings holding rich tartan cloth napkins. It was a heady mixture of wealth and British culture. As she placed the Sheikh's plate down and pulled away from the table, she was suddenly grabbed by the wrist, forcing her against the seated man. Not knowing what to do, she tried to pull away but felt the grip tighten, so much so that she began to wince. Noticing Bernadine's expression, Mr Wilks, who sat opposite, cleared his throat and said,

"Mr Sheikh Mohamed Imran Sir, I believe you are a keen golfer?"

The Sheikh dropped Bernadine's small wrist, then looked at her in such a way as to say, 'What are you hanging about here for? Away you go!'

"The golf? Ah yes. It is a hobby of mine, sir. I hope you will take me to the golfing here. There is one course here I love to see."

Bernadine quickly made for the door. It was only when she was halfway down the corridor back to the kitchen that she allowed herself to rub her tender wrist. She felt awfully violated and her heart hammered against her chest. She forced herself to take slow, deep breaths. Maybe she had been provocative somehow; maybe she had startled him and he'd grabbed her wrist in shock. Why did Mr Wilks come to her aid then? Had she lingered at the table too long when she leaned in to place the dishes down? Her head swam.

Charlotte was drenched in sweat. The industrial dishwasher blew plumes of hot steam at her when she opened it to retrieve the plates. The large sink was full of used bowls and dishes, and the scrapings bin overflowed. Mr Romano shouted through the kitchen chute to be careful as he was sending through the sharp kitchen knives. He followed these with a few pans that were so burnt they would need to be steeped and scrubbed. Three other red shirts, including

Jasmine worked their way through the lot in the intense heat. It was too noisy to talk and they were already 15 minutes into their recreation time. Finally, the last tray of cutlery was dried, polished and replaced in the tray so the four red shirts could be dismissed. Charlotte felt like a child being released for playtime.

"Let's go Jas! Let's gooooo!!!"

Hooking Jasmine's arm around hers, she made a playful skip down the corridor, the two young women managed to maintain their playful skipping for several metres before going out of sync and releasing each other in a fit of giggles. The two other red shirts hissed at Charlotte and Jasmine to shut up or they'd jeopardise the rest of recreation time. They slowed to a more formal walk just in the nick of time as one of the doors opened in the corridor and two men walked out.

Jasmine recognised one as the chief of security but couldn't place the other. The red shirts nodded politely and let them go ahead. Charlotte afforded her red-shirted comrades a grateful nod as she shuddered to think about what would have happened if she and Jasmine had been caught only moments before.

Right at the end of the corridor where the Praise group paintings had usually hung was a large new, rather intense portrait of the Sheikh. He must have looked directly at the artist as he painted him as the eyes seemed to follow the small red group around the corridor. Charlotte found it rather unnerving. Poor Bernadine felt her skin crawl.

Chapter 15

Pat, deep in thought, pulled the tiny weeds that webbed themselves around the succulents on the rockery. She loved the scent of the earth, the herb garden, the wild areas and the neat vegetable allotments. When she had been younger and new to the Abbey, she had been central to the planning and development of many of the sites that now flourished with mature foliage and boasted the spoils of an English country garden.

She threw the last few weeds into the bucket, stretched up and gently twisted her back to ease its strain. Looking briefly in all directions to check she was quite alone, she reached into the pocket of her raincoat and pulled out her cigarettes. Choosing a particularly large and stable looking rock, she sat down and lit up.

Over in the distance, she could see people at the tennis courts, there was a new spectators stand in progress and the distant high-vis yellow jackets and red shirts gave an impression of wildflowers moving about in the breeze. The red shirts were poppies, she supposed.

She blew a cloud of grey smoke towards them as her thoughts habitually drifted to her pre-Abbey days. Many years ago, she had lived a miserable life of filth and poverty. By her late teens, she was solely responsible for bringing up her twin half-brothers and older yet mentally younger sister. Her mother had finally killed herself with an accidental overdose when Pat was at school. After a year or so, the twins were taken into care and the older sister applied to the council to get a house as she was 3 months pregnant. Prior to her mother's death, Pat had cut out an existence on the miserable estate. The tenement flat the family had lived in was on the top floor and without a lift, Pat had to pull herself up six sets of concrete steps to get home. The McGregors on the first floor put out a nice door mat that said 'welcome,' which seemed pretty ironic as they were the most unwelcoming pompous bunch Pat had ever come across. When Mrs McGregor tutted condescendingly at Pat and her family, she would deliberately rub her muddy feet right across the 'welcome' on their mat, then she'd bolt upstairs and turn the key.

Lonely Mr Dunn never came out other than when the street lamps were on. The Charlton family always played loud music, then the Zagrib family across the way seemed to have half a dozen partially dressed small infants wandering about at any given time. The other flats had so many changes of occupants that Pat gave up trying to learn their names.

There was a red brick church built right in the centre of the estate with nettles and graffiti nearly covering one wall around by the large wheelie bin. The druggies used to inject heroin by the overflowing black sacks; it was a well-known no-go area for the local kids. At the worst of times, Patricia had to go there with her sister to find her mother and haul her back home up the tenement steps. The twins bawled till their eyes were raw and their cheeks glistened with tears and slime. The only plug to stop the noise was to lay their semi-conscious mother across the bed so they could curl up beside her to sleep. It was terrible.

Pat closed her eyes and tried hard to listen to the sounds around her. She could hear a blackbird crying out its alarm call. Maybe one of the Abbey cats was nearby. There were shouts from the tennis courts and the lovely 'poc poc' sound of the ball hitting the rackets. She took a deep drag, the small orangey glow crept a few millimetres up the cigarette. The horses were out in the paddocks, swishing their tails to keep away the flies. There was one red dot onboard a distant horse and another red dot mounting up. Heavenly.

Just as Pat extinguished her cigarette, two shadows approached. It was Mr Compton and Mother Pascal.

"Still smoking those horrible things?" came the not too friendly greeting from Pascal.

"They ain't too 'orrible to me."

Mr Compton extended a hand to help Pat up from the large rock and marvelled at how she sprang up effortlessly.

"We were heading over to the refectory Pat and wondered if you wished to join us. I can sign off your last 30 minutes. I think you were pretty much done for today anyway.

"A gardener ain't ever done, Mr Compton," said Pat, looking regretfully at the borders. She nodded obediently though and promised to meet them there once she'd returned the bucket and her gardening gloves. She had learned early on at the Abbey that implied suggestions were actually orders and must be followed at all times.

The large garden house was full of activity; newer red shirts were learning the ropes from the more experienced gardeners. They were tending to the indoor plants, filling tiny seed trays, and studying something seemingly fascinating on their tablets. As she placed her gloves in her small locker, she noticed Charlotte and Tilly right over at the tomatoes, deep in discussion.

"Pat!"

"Whassup young uns?" She raised an eyebrow at Charlotte and Tilly, who were approaching.

"Have you a minute, Pat? We've a bit of an idea."

Charlotte had that daft look she so often sported when she was up to something. Pat had come to associate that look with trouble.

"I've been ordered to go down to the refectory. I ain't got time m'loves. I'll 'ave to catch you later."

With barely a look behind, Pat made her way to Mother Pascal and Charlotte's father. Anticipating a conversation relating to Charlotte, she didn't want her nonsense right at the forefront of her head in case she let slip that she thought the young woman was a reckless walking disaster.

Contrary to her expectations, Mr Compton barely mentioned his daughter and instead told Pat of a sudden, sad decline in the health of Mr Edward Stramford, founder of the Abbey. This news, although not altogether unexpected, did sit heavily on Pat and she took a moment to let it sink in.

"He's got a few months at most, Pat. It could be less."

"Oh... I see."

"He didn't want any interventions other than pain relief... you know... in line with his beliefs, of course."

"Yeah, I know," Pat felt her hands shaking slightly, so she joined them firmly in her lap and watched some red shirts queuing at the door, ready to file in for their lunch.

Mr Wilks walked past them and pulled out his phone, only to glance at it before replacing it in his pocket. They were in a seating area outside the refectory so that they could talk, though Pat felt her words shrivelling up like the weeds she'd pulled earlier... curling and drying in her bucket.

"He has actually asked to see you, Pat."

"He 'as?"

"Yes. He has also requested that you are with him at the end to provide end of life care."

"Course."

The red shirts disappeared through the doors. There was a distant exclamation from Mr Romano in the kitchens and the sounds of plates and crockery. Mother Pascal, who had sat silently, finally cleared her throat.

"You are to undertake additional prayer sessions each morning over the time you would have choir. Your usual duties will be adjusted to allow for you to care for Mr Stramford accordingly. I believe Bernadine will be there too, as well as Jasmine. I will need the three of you to report to me daily."

"Course."

The Abbey bells chimed once and Pat wondered if it was one or half past the hour. What state would Mr Stramford be in? Would he even know his prognosis? How long did he have? It was all so sudden.

Mr Compton and Pascal took their leave. Pat continued to sit on the cushioned seating. The thought of lunch made her stomach knot uncomfortably. If Mr Stramford died, who would run the Abbey? There were less and less of the old crew, and over the years, she had disappeared into the workforce and the running of the place became ever more mysterious. Without doubt, she mused this was her favourite place to exist and through all the years, she had slowly laid her demons to rest, accepting her jail and even feeling some gratitude knowing that whenever her time was up, she would never suffer the drawn-out physical pain and humiliation she so associated with the conventional end of life care.

Mr Stramford lay propped on pillows so that the vegetable gardens could be seen through the window. A number of old books were stacked by his bedside, along with reading glasses and an engraved fountain pen. He stirred for a few moments and managed a throaty whisper, whereupon Jasmine immediately came over. Words were amalgamated with wheezing and laboured breaths, finally managing to say a few words, including 'Pat'. A coughing episode took over. Jasmine gave him water and cooled his forehead with sterile cloths.

"I'm 'ere sir."

He recovered enough to move his head to face Pat, who had taken Jasmine's chair.

"I need a moment of your time Pat."

"Of course sir, I'm 'ere."

"I am on the way out Pat. I'm sure you can see that." He cracked a smile and his old eyes twinkled. "That's not to say I'm content to be departing this early on in the journey... but what will be will be."

She studied him. He had become gaunt with whatever mysterious illness ravished him. His hair was pure white, though still as thick as the day she had met him at that church... all those years ago.

"I wanted to speak to you, particularly Pat. I've no time to do this properly... circumstances have rushed me rather and it reminds me that our own agendas can never take priority over almighty God."

The old man's voice had become congested with phlegm and he took a moment to recover.

He continued...

"You, Pat encompass all the Abbey stands for. It flows through your veins, the power to care for people. The warmth of God."

"It was your kindness sir, all them years ago..."

"It wasn't me Pat, I'm just the messenger. God taught me to love. He taught me to care for those in need irrespective of their circumstances, Pat. The tears of the hot-headed daughter of a billionaire are still tears..." He paused, and swallowed...

"It's all relative..." His eyes scrunched together momentarily, then opened and found Pat again.

"Pain is pain Pat, that's why this place is so important. It enables me as a Christian to try to heal others' pain, in a..." He paused, talking hurt him.

"If we can teach the most entitled, arrogant, wealthy people to recognize a shared human characteristic...that of the need to care and be cared... for."

He had to squeak out the last word as his lungs would not cooperate. Pat felt tears welling in her eyes. She was not one to cry. Why did this hugely influential and powerful man want to share his last words with her? She looked at the burst capillaries in his cheeks, the way his eyebrows were thick with long hairs curling into his fringe. He was just a man with hair, bones and blood.

"It's about love, ain't it, sir? It's about showin' people that we can all function together, right? We can grow to 'ave enough respect for each other to keep the Abbey goin'"

Mr Stramford smiled.

"Yes, Pat, it's exactly that. Look long into our human history, our wealthy and powerful leaders have sought to 'manage' the poor, the needy and so on. What the Abbey does...or what I hope it does... is give a different perspective to those wealthier souls who have lost their way, who have become greedy, selfish and so on..."

The coughing started again. Jasmine appeared with water but was refused.

"Take them out of society... teach them to care for one another and leave the poorest and neediest to find their own solutions... through community, through the church, through the human spirit... do you understand Pat? Do you see that the people that come to the Abbey are more in need of rehabilitation than anyone... for the good of wider society as well as themselves?"

Pat's heart hammered. She remembered his strong hands clasping her shoulders when tears rolled uncontrollably down her teenage face.

"I wanna be good, I wanna be like you lot, I hate my life, I hate the sufferin' Take me into your world, take me with you."

The old man lay back into the pillows and rested his eyes, though Pat knew he was not asleep. Bernadine was preparing the next dose of morphine under the watchful eye of Jasmine.

"Sir?"

Mr Stramford opened his eyes.

"How will the Abbey carry on without you?"

"I hope Pat, that the Abbey will continue to deliver adult education, so rooted in care... that future generations will govern societies worldwide... focusing not on wealth, capitalism and power, but health, sustainability and love."

He shut his eyes and his face contorted as discomfort spasmed through him.

"This world has plenty for everybody. With the correct mindset, people will champion love rather than wealth... and selfishness will be shunned in favour of kindness. Do you see Pat? Do you see how the Abbey is the seed of change... society needs?"

Pat felt herself lighten as if her spirit had started to lift away from her mortal body. "But sir, why are you telling all this to me? Ain't you gonna tell all this stuff to the Sheikh? He's takin' over ain't he? What's the good of tellin' me?"

The old man did not open his eyes. He lay completely still. At last, his chest raised and fell and his lips trembled. Pat leaned in close as Mr Stramford whispered his final words.

"I believe God watches you."

Chapter 16

At prayers, Charlotte would allow her thoughts to wander back to the days of watching late night films, drinking cheap whisky and coke, and munching away on fistfuls of toffee covered popcorn and Doritos. The cheesy residue on the corners of her mouth, left for her tongue to rediscover later. She would leave the curtains shut all day and slide about the house in her pyjamas, braless and soulless. Now, things were very different. The rigid timetable, the outdoor pursuits, nature, the kitchen work, and the endless Bible study with the constant emphasis on caring, caring for each other, caring for those in need, care, care, care. Charlotte had learnt the hard way that shouting,

"I don't care, I don't give a flying fuck!"

When in a rage about something resulted in occasional physical punishment, but usually a stint in solitary. She noticed with some repulsion that Mother Pascal clenched her jaw with a strange satisfaction as she gazed trance like at Charlotte, fending off the slaps and fists of Wilks.

Charlotte knew she could be reckless at times and often emotive, but she felt nothing justified such a physical system of order. Surely, this was supposed to be a progressive place of healing based on the Christian faith. Physical brutality was as regressive as it got. Didn't Jesus tell an angry mob that he, without sin should cast the first stone at the condemned woman? Charlotte was no monster, careless maybe, but a thrill seeker, yes probably. It was her way of taking control of her new life, to question the rules, to rebel, and to feel alive.

Slightly late out of choir, Charlotte broke into a light run to the refectory for lunch. Pushing open the door, she saw with some relief that many red shirts were still taking their seats. Spotting Jasmine, taller than most, she headed over. Mealtimes were always silent, but this silence was thicker than usual. Even Mr Romano seemed to be creeping quietly about the kitchen. She looked around her and saw the whole staff cohort were present, though subdued. The tension was unnerving. Feeling the all too familiar lightness of adrenaline entering her veins, she made a decision to wait, put her head down, and wait.

Her pulse increased, heightening her senses as the blood coursed around her body... She could feel Bernadine to her left shaking in a badly contained state of inner turmoil. To her right, Jasmine sat upright, strong and controlled, her dipped head suggesting she was as alert and suspicious as Charlotte. The food had not yet appeared in the canteen area, which was not unusual. What was unusual, however, is that Mother Pascal, the leader of pre-meal prayers was nowhere to be seen.

From the back of the hall, the door opened and the Sheikh entered, instantly recognisable in his distinctive robes. He was flanked by four armed men, presumably his security team. The panel of suits who usually stood to inspect and maintain order over the refectory, were seated in a similar fashion to the red shirts. Charlotte recognised her father as well as Mr Wilks and wondered at their demeanour. A speaker's stand was produced and the Sheikh climbed the two steps up, now towering over the smart military looking Asian man who stood beside him. He spoke and the translator began...

"Ladies and gentlemen, it is with deep sorrow that the Honourable Sheikh Mohamed Imran announces the death of Sir Edward Stramford, founder and chairman of this great institution, The Stramford Abbey. A formal death notice will be filed by noon tomorrow and the funeral will commence within the week. Here at the Abbey, we will be holding a service of remembrance tomorrow afternoon. This takes full precedence over any planned activities, and we require a full congregation and choir. Regarding code of dress, Gentlemen, you will be suited and ladies will have full head coverings out of respect for the late Mr Stramford."

The translator took a moment to confer with the Sheikh before continuing.

"From this moment on, the Abbey becomes the property of Mr Sheikh Mohamed Imran and a number of changes are to be implemented with immediate effect. Full details of these will be available to you on the devices we will be allocating to you by this afternoon. Device training will begin at point of delivery and a dedicated ICT station, located adjacent to the library, will be open at all times for device maintenance and repair. Mr Stramford was a great man with a considerable heart. He formed a strong friendship with the Great Sheikh Mohamed Imran and it was his dying wish that his institution should fall into his capable hands. Let it be known that the Abbey remains unchanged in its purpose, that of care and compassion to the most vulnerable and forgotten in our society."

"Where's Pascal?" Charlotte snatched a whisper.

Jasmine kept her lips entirely still but managed to hiss.

"I think something's up."

"How serious?" "Very."

The speaker's eyes swept over their table like a searchlight. Charlotte pressed her thumb hard against her wrist, a tactic she often used to stop her face betraying her. Eyes cast down demurely, the women ceased discussion.

Within hours, the full cohort had collected a device and a pack of clothing wrapped in thin plastic. The clothing was a simple charcoal grey suit for all the men and a long-sleeved black tunic for the women with a grey headscarf. 30 minutes was allocated to change in the cabins and meet in the newly constructed lecture theatre over at the science block.

"So, as well as being incarcerated against our will, we're being forcibly converted to Islam…" Charlotte took on an exaggeratedly jovial tone as she shook out her jeans and folded them on the chair, the red polo shirt receiving a similar shake,

"Never thought I'd miss this scarlet wonder."

"Well, it makes a nice change, I suppose. I wasn't a particularly good Christian anyway... you never know Charlotte, you might make an excellent Muslim."

"Enough!" Bernadine screeched so uncharacteristically that the two women stopped and stared in complete silence. "How can you make such a mockery of all this? It is terrible, it is obscene... I cannot... I will not." She wavered, eyes brimming, cheeks flaring.

"Hey come on, Bernadine, we're not mocking anything... but ourselves." Bernadine's long hair fell over her shoulder as she brushed it furiously, catching it in a low tail, she put on the grey headscarf. Her hands found each other and clasped together, which seemed to calm her as she took several slow, deep breaths.

Charlotte and Jasmine exchanged glances but said nothing.

"Come on, you lot!" Pat's voice snapped from outside the door.

"You're gettin' close to bein' late."

The four women fast-walked across the forecourt and then one broke free, sprinting full dash back to the cabin to pick up her forgotten device. The run had felt good though and Charlotte was glad to feel her heart hammering against her chest.

The huge cohort were lectured for a solid two hours on the basic functions of their devices. They were all programmed with schedules and alarms for each work slot or activity they had done previously, but there was a tracker inside each device which showed where each person was against a map of the Abbey. Charlotte's screen showed a swarm of flashing dots in the science block, but her thoughts wandered to where Mother Pascal's flashing dot might be. She also wondered whether she was feeling brave enough to ask the lecturer whether the patients were tracked as well as the carers but thought better of it.

It was made very clear to the whole cohort that every device could be scrutinised to ensure that it was being used properly, every action and input was logged and could be accessed at any time. There was a section for carers to make notes on all their patients and there was scope for ICT jobs within the establishment for those who showed a flair for concise device-based logs and time management.

The timetable could be changed from weekly to a more detailed daily schedule. The device would automatically check in and out as the device owner completed their daily tasks. The devices were to be kept on the person at all times in a specially adapted pocket in the lapels of the men's jacket and in an internal pocket in the ladies' tunic. Only in exceptional circumstances could the device be removed from the pocket and placed in one of the many

secured lockers on the premises. Finally, the session drew to a close with a barked "Any questions?"

Charlotte raised her hand.

Jasmine and Pat, both independently of each other, raised their eyes to the heavens.

"What if you lose the device?"

"There is no scope here to lose your device. When partaking in sports or activities that require physical exertion, the device is to be placed in one of the lockers located at every station, otherwise it will stay in your tunic."

"What if you went for a walk or something and it fell out of your pocket?"

"Then you would stoop down and pick... it... up." The translator narrowed his eyes. Jasmine risked thumping her friend on the thigh to stop her continuing.

"Thank you, that is most... informative."

"Any further questions?"

There were none.

Praise group was quiet. The music was off, the clatter of coffee cups was null. The only sounds that remained were the sporadic ticks of some of the more vocal patients. The praise group staff whispered conspiratorially with heads bowed. Charlotte tried to differentiate the grey pillars and suits to determine who was who. Jasmin was easy as she was so tall, the others were altogether more ambiguous. The beautiful long plait of the Chinese lady was hidden completely and Charlotte missed it.

The paintings were being removed and replaced with beautiful mosaic- like tiles. Posters with smiley faces and phonics were replaced with scripted letters and numbers.

Pat appeared and beckoned Charlotte, who left Tilly with her silk paints to follow her. Through the small corridor, she reached Michael's private bedchamber. The door was ajar and Charlotte noticed that Pat had pulled off her headscarf and was seated opposite Michael as he rocked gently on the side of his bed.

"Take that thing off your 'ead and come 'ere quick. This lad is fadin' on me."

Charlotte saw Pat's eyes were rimmed pink and new tears glistened threateningly.

"Pat!"

Charlotte was shocked. This woman embodied the 'keep calm and carry on', tough British stoicism and yet here she was, completely crestfallen.

"I can't get through to 'im. He don't smile at me no more. He just stares like that."

Charlotte took her eyes away from her friend and looked at Michael. He looked much the same as he ever did.

"He looks alright Pat. Maybe you need to have a bit of a break yourself? Can I cover for you? Shall I call Mother Pascal?"

"I dunno where that wuman even is Charlotte, she's all but disappeared."

"D'you need a minute? I'll cover for you. Leave your tablet in here and go have a smoke out the bathroom window."

"Aw love, it ain't me. It's this boy. He's lost his soul. It's killin' me. I've bin carin' for 'im since he came ere, just 18 he was."

Charlotte made a mental note of how that did not correlate with the narrative both women had entered the Abbey together, but she did not comment.

"I've seen 'im smile. I've held 'is hand... watched him grow. I think it's the end. His mum'll be in pieces. I'll be lost without 'im. He's the constant that's kept me goin'"

Charlotte knelt at the feet of the small man and gently took his hands. He stopped rocking but did not look at her.

With a gentle squeeze of his hand, she began a quiet hum. An old Irish tune, simplistic yet haunting. Charlotte knew her voice stirred emotion. She often felt a quiet surge of joy as she gathered the sound from deep within her diaphragm, the vibrations gentle on her sternum.

Pat quietly but quickly moved to his door and shut it with a click, next to the window, as if the voice and its healing powers might escape, wasted in the breeze.

Michael slowly, awkwardly stood. Charlotte turned the hum to voice. Michael turned away from the women and with some difficulty, pulled back his bed clothes. One knee at a time, he knelt into the mattress, slowly twisting himself round until he lay, head on the pillow slightly to the left so he could settle his eyes on Pat. He looked from Pat to Charlotte, Charlotte to Pat. Then, a slow unsteady smile broke across his lips. His eyes stopped darting between the two and instead settled on Pat, eventually flickering closed as if to conclude the meeting.

Charlotte quietened to a hum once more and gently finished her song.

Michael's chest rose and fell.

Chapter 17

Bim sat at the kitchen table, not fully free from the clutches of sleep. His eyes felt heavy and his shoulders stiff. Clicking his fingers one by one, he felt the release as each knuckle popped. A cantering of feet hailed the arrival of their cat. Bim watched as the animal misjudged the slippy tiles causing the fluffy rear to collide into the front paws. With the utmost dignity, the cat swiftly recovered and with an indignant swish of his tail, sailed up in a graceful arc. Landing centimetres from the coffee pot, he pushed his velvet nose under his master's hand. Bim cast a furtive glance behind him and finding the coast was clear, indulged the cat in some under chin scratching migrating behind the ears. A great whirring and purring came forth, overriding the approaching footsteps from the hall.

"Good grief Bim, why don't you just go all the way and give him a place setting!"

The cat, who was helping himself to the milk jug, stopped guiltily and hastily vacated the scene. Bim feigned innocence, claiming the incident could only have happened as he looked the other way, but while she was near the bread bin, he'd love another croissant.

"They're nice these." Pauline remarked, halving hers with barely an escaped crumb. "From that new patisserie, aren't they?"

"I think so love," replied her husband as his croissant expelled clouds of crumbs across side-plate, placemat and tablecloth.

The couple ate their breakfast peacefully, commenting on the day ahead, the weather, the cat. It was only when the urgent message arrived on both phones that a great leaden cloud descended. The change in the two bright figures was immediate, they became rigid as adrenaline took hold. They had prepared for this day ever since they had learnt of their son's terrible prognosis, yet here they were flailing in no man's land.

"This is it."

"We have to go now."

"Oh Bim, I don't think I can stand it."

"I've got you love."

The two held each other until Pauline broke away and began to gather her keys, her phone, and her handbag. Her hair was not done, her feet were slippered, remnants of croissant sat in stodgy lumps between her teeth. She caught her grey face in the mirror, it scared her.

"Darling, please take a minute. They will be taking good care of him. He will be comfortable."

"There's no time, we have to leave now."

Pauline continued to circle listlessly around the kitchen, searching for something she did not know. Bim stayed still and placed his head in his hands. It was most probable the Abbey had timed this call to fit with his schedule. Perhaps Michael had been half dead for the last four days and they'd waited until now. Sunday, the sacred day. Their day together. It wasn't that he would miss Michael so much, perhaps more the loss of his title. 'Father.' There had been times where Michael had seemed almost like every other child, sat in a swing as a toddler. Bumbling along to the nursery with his little blue backpack, woolly mittens in the snow, a plastic sledge and rosy cheeks.

Bim had found some parts of fatherhood pleasant. The early years, Michael looked similar to the other children at the nursery, though he could not speak. He took an age to toilet train and further still to communicate. Pauline had strived to 'fix' Michael in every way she knew how, though she never received affection or even a smile of recognition... When he was three then four, she spent hours with various paediatric consultants who devised numerous plans for his welfare, though they seldom took account of Pauline's welfare and Bim saw his wife spiral into debilitating exhaustion and despair. At five, Michael was taken into a highly exclusive fee-paying boarding school where his complex needs were addressed through counselling and regular therapy sessions. By the time he was 15, he had all but departed from the lives of his parents (save the occasional 'relaxed and informal' meeting.)

Finally, the black car rumbled up to the gates. Pauline grew impatient at the driver, why was he so damned slow?! Why was every traffic light red? Why were birds continuing to sing?

The familiar shapes of Mr Wilks, Mr Compton and the young nun Bernadine stood at the entrance as the car came to a stop. Unable to wait for the driver to open her door, Pauline was out of the car and across the gravel driveway. Impatient for Bim to follow, she exchanged generic greetings and enquired of the young Bernadine as to where Mother Pascal was. She seemed unable to give any sort of definitive answer.

The party descended upon the small room which had Michael's personal belongings displayed as if in a boutique. Pauline noticed the small car she had given to him on their last visit. He wore blue silk pyjamas and seemed to be sleeping peacefully, though on closer inspection, she could see that he was covered in cannulas and drips had been tastefully hidden behind the headboard. Only the heart monitor was visible as a doctor looked on.

"Where is Heather? Where is Heather Pascal?"

"Madam, I apologise but she has taken ill."

"That's unfortunate. Would she accept a visit? I feel I really must see her."

"As I said Madam, I regretfully must inform you that she is declining all visitors."

Pauline felt peculiar. This scene had played multiple times in her mind, each time with Heather by her side. Now everything felt barren, the young nun there to comfort and guide looked barely older than a child.

Taking a seat beside her son, she took his hand in hers. It was limp and cool and the tape from the cannula stole much of his thin wrist. Bim motioned for the party to leave him, his wife and son some privacy.

Pat sat on one of the large soap crates in the laundry room. She looked about at the industrial sized bottles of disinfectant, toilet rolls and medical supplies. Tilting up her chin, she exhaled a deep sigh towards the open skylight. Her tablet vibrated with a notification, she had been called to Michael's room to meet with the prime minister and his wife. She had not envisaged this, she was always supposed to be working in the background, with Mother Pascal, the face of the Abbey, giving the Prime minister and his wife detailed updates as to his condition coupled with spiritual support and care. He was here to die, that was always understood, and it was the Abbey's job to ensure it was as painless and pleasant as possible. So why did Pat feel unease creeping about under her skin. Where was Pascal?

The buzzing little dictator could wait. Once this boy died, and die he would, Pat knew she would experience that same suffocating hopelessness of her youth. She would have to learn how to breathe again.

The death of Mr Stramford, though sudden, was expected, but the safety net of his legacy left her resolute and determined to care for young Michael. "God watches you," he said. Was He watching this?

The buzz continued aggressively. If Pat didn't pick up soon, the buzz would turn to an alarm, loud and insatiable. Finally, she leapt down from the crate and made her way to Michael's bed chamber.

"Mr Nkosi, sir... madam." Pat nodded politely as she found them separated. The mother stooped by her son's bedside. The father stood looking out of the small window. The doctor busied herself with the medicines behind the screen.

"How long has he been like this?" Mrs Nkosi asked calmly.

"He ain't uncomfortable madam, but he ain't got much strength left either. He's gettin' weaker."

Pat looked to the doctor for support, though she was absorbed, scribbling notes.

"He won' know when the time comes, he's completely sedated."

"But how long?"

"It's 'ard to say. Today? Tomorrow? It depends 'ow long 'is body…" Pat trailed off, she suddenly remembered who she was speaking to and felt overwhelmed.

"Do you know how Heather Pascal is? I know it's brutish to insist upon seeing her, but I really…" Pauline too, tailed off.

"Come now darling, we must respect Mother Pascal's condition. This lady is not in a position to tell us… I'm sorry, Patricia, you're Patricia, aren't you? My wife has been used to the near continuous presence of Mother Pascal throughout young Michael's stay here."

"Of course, sir, I quite understand."

A silence took hold, save the scribbling pencil. Pat began fussing with the cup and water jug on the bedside table, rearranging the small pile of books and toys. Quite suddenly, Bim walked to the door. "I'm just going to take a little air dear. Will you be ok?"

Pauline nodded without looking at him.

Pat stood rather awkwardly. She knew she was a shoddy alternative to Mother Pascal, the caregiver of the church, the long-term friend of this powerful woman. She wished she could draw upon psalms and prayers to help, but she feared forgetting the words or worse, bursting into tears.

The door clicked shut.

"Doctor? Please can you also leave us for a moment?"

Obligingly, the doctor nodded at Mrs Nkosi and left too. Pat, now feeling very uncertain, moved to go also but found a hand upon her forearm.

"Please don't be afraid of me Patricia. I am just a woman like you and though you're not Heather, I know you share a great love for my boy."

Pat followed the gaze of the mother to her son and noted how even his features were. His black hair so like his father but his complexion much paler and more akin to his mother. But this was odd. Why had she dismissed the doctor? Always, people moved in pairs, in groups. It was a security habit. Why did she want to be alone with her?

"I ain't afraid madam, only that I could possibly make things worse. I dunno what to say to be honest. I mean, I liked your boy."

Pat transferred her weight from foot to foot.

"Would... would a prayer help?"

Pauline shook her head with a small smile.

"No Patricia, I just want to speak to someone, someone who has spent time with my son, not someone who is promoting this establishment as an investable business opportunity..." She quietened, as if spilling her thoughts had been accidental, "but a woman... such as you, with a heart... such as yours."

The two women sat on either side of Michael. Pat, though uncomfortable, realised what this mother needed and obliged as well as she could with various anecdotes from Michael's young adult life, from pottery, to simple tennis, to riding... oh how he loved the horses in his stronger days. How the horses seemed to sense his frailty and take extra care when he was on board. The toy cars he ordered into colours and sizes, his favourite purple monster truck with the huge wheels he took to bed and hid under his pillow.

Pauline smiled and chuckled at times, her admiration quietly building that such a roughly spoken grey lady like this should know her son so deeply, so well.

"And finally..." Pauline said, sweeping away a tear with a tissue.

"I want to know about you, you and the other staff here. I want to know how things are."

The door opened abruptly and both the doctor and a new face walked in. She was tall and in Islamic traditional dress. Her face was beautiful.

"Madam Nkosi. I apologise for the delay in getting to you. With dear Mother Pascal unwell, I have been sent in her absence."

The two ladies shook hands and Pat was dismissed.

173

The Stramford room, now replete with ornate, beautiful Middle Eastern furniture, buzzed with conversation and ripples of polite laughter. A formal drinks evening was in full flow and Bernadine, Charlotte and Jasmine went from group to group, refilling glasses and offering trays of Mr Romanos' finest canapes. The vast majority of the guests were male and wearing expensive dinner suits, save the Prime Ministers wife, Lady Nkosi and the beautiful Islamic lady who Pauline now knew to be the Sheikh's personal advisor. Scheduled was a series of lectures from both the Sheikh and the British chief of security, punctuated with further canapes and drinks and an opportunity for the guests to circulate and create networks. The theme of the evening was The Abbey and its exponential growth.

As the evening progressed, the atmosphere became increasingly charged with testosterone. The aftereffects of the first lecture seemed to manifest themselves in a sort of mass bullish entitlement. This resulted in finger clicking to attract the waitress's attention, over friendly pats and leery comments. By the time Charlotte made it to Mrs Nkosi, she could see the lady was struggling to keep her composure as something so obviously bothered her.

"Madam? Can I…. can I help you?"

Bim Nkosi was deep in discussion with two men who seemed to hang intently to his every word. Pauline however, stared into the middle distance, obviously hurting.

Charlotte tried again.

"Madam?"

"Yes, might I be excused, Bim? I wish to see Michael."

"Of course, love."

The two women left the party. Another of the Abbey's staff was notified on her tablet that she was needed in the Stramford room to cover for Charlotte.

Pauline Nkosi's shoes clattered across the stone floors of the Abbey as she marched forward almost militarily, anxious to get away from the other guests, to get away from the noise.

"Madam, are you ok?"

Pauline stopped abruptly and turned to face Charlotte.

"I'm not ok, no, not really. I'm struggling here. I have to say, I really could have done with seeing Heather... but she is apparently unreachable, I'm being fed with alternatives. What the actual hell is going on here? Do you know? Does anyone know?"

The small woman let out a cry of exasperation.

"I'm sorry... I don't know what's gotten into me."

Charlotte, without thinking took the lady's wrists in her hands.

"Look, I'm probably speaking massively out of turn here, but as I understand it, you're grieving for your kid, which must be absolutely soul destroying. Your best friend who's always been there for you has inexplicably buggered off without a trace and to top it all off, you've been wrestled into a cocktail evening with a bunch of leery bastards all wanking each other off, metaphorically of course, while they collectively decide the fate of this place... and us all... obviously."

Pauline blinked. A tremble of a smile came and quickly went.

"I think perhaps we should talk."

"I can't. I can only take you to Michael and then go back to the party."

"Right."

The two ladies walked on in silence, past the Abbey and through the old graveyard. Eventually, as they neared the doors to the building, Pauline stopped. Taking out her phone, she began typing out a messageand then, as she sent it, she began.

"I need to talk to you about my spiritual needs, and sadly, I cannot connect with the dear Sheikh's spiritual adviser at this time. I have excused you for the next hour."

The words came calmly, but as Charlotte looked at Pauline's face, she appeared to be trying to communicate with her silently. It was hard to determine what she meant, only a mouthed "off the record."

"That's fine," replied Charlotte, perplexed. Pauline was shining with perspiration, not from exertion but from apparent fear.

There followed a series of pointed looks at the tablet in Charlotte's tunic. "Can I suggest, Mrs Nkosi, that we take some time in the Abbey for some quiet reflection?"

"I... I would be most grateful." Came the voice, but the eyes shone.

The two ladies walked into the Abbey to find they were quite alone, save two men cleaning the choir stalls with a pleasantly scented wood polish.

"Come, put your tablet in the locker here, with my phone. It is the height of bad manners to use them here."

Charlotte obeyed and the two ladies moved to the chapel, selecting a pew near the back. They sat together and bowed their heads respectfully.

"I think we cannot be heard here."

"Why? What's going on?" Charlotte looked at Pauline but was hissed a command to look to the front.

"Talk we must, but if we are seen to be in a deep discussion, suspicions will build."

"Ok, ok, of course." Charlotte noticed her legs were much longer than Mrs Nkosi's as her knees nearly touched the pew in front. There was the familiar book of hymns in front, and on the altar, a single candle burned.

"There is something well wrong here, Charlotte. I arrived here expecting to bury my dead son, but instead, I have seen things so concerning that I feel I already know too much. I feel we could be in significant danger."

Charlotte, head bowed, felt her stomach tense. "Go on"

"You've been here for some months now, I understand? I think you are rebellious. I've heard that. Because of that, you may be my best hope."

"I'm sorry, what are you getting at?"

"I've seen something of the illusive Mother Pascal."

Pauline paused to take a tissue from her handbag.

"I believe I was meant to see her to alleviate any suspicions I may have had about her whereabouts, but what they do not know is how close I was to that woman and how I know her so well."

"Ok, so where was she?"

"At the drinks party, before you and the other waitresses were there, she appeared with Mr Wilks. The two of them walked right beside Bim, and me, and Mr Wilks made an exaggerated gesture towards me, whereupon she waved."

"Ok, so…"

"Heather doesn't bloody wave Charlotte!" Pauline hissed, exasperated at Charlotte's slow uptake. "The two walked straight over to a table of guests and sat with their backs to us, apparently engaging in conversation of a most… jovial nature."

"I'm sorry, I'm just not following you."

"It wasn't her, Charlotte. It was a fraud. A very good one, I'll admit, but it was not Heather Pascal. I know that woman's mannerisms and foibles. I know she cannot wave the way she did last night…"

"Why not?"

"Because of an old horse riding injury which puts her elbow at a peculiar angle, but the point is. The point is Charlotte, that I was meant to be fooled."

"Why didn't you go up to her?"

"Because before I could head over, she appeared to make her excuses to the table and with a very uncharacteristic smile in my direction, left the room, again with Mr Wilks. I tried to break away from the group I was in, but they became almost forceful in holding me in conversation so that, save bolting after her, I could not reasonably leave."

Mrs Nkosi took her lipstick from the front pocket of her handbag and applied a layer.

"It was only when you all arrived with your canopies that the mood lightened enough that I could make some excuse to go."

Charlotte noticed Pauline was trembling.

"So, what do you want me to do?"

"I believe that the real Heather Pascal may be being held somewhere here, though I don't know why. I think something very serious is going on here since the death of Mr Stramford. I'd... I'd go as far as to say that I suspect the Abbey is being used for an entirely different purpose than what was intended. Maybe she cottoned on. She was always very astute."

"What purpose? Surely, you have suspicions. Do you think your husband knows?"

"I think he is party to it, but I believe he and many others have been sold a story convincing enough to invest in."

The two ladies fell silent as the entrance door banged, footsteps could be heard as one of the stable lads walked into the chapel and took a pew at the very front.

Charlotte breathed her quietest whisper,

"How can you be so sure? What evidence have you got other than your intuition?"

Pauline did not reply immediately.

"Other than out of a Christian desire to help people, why else does this place exist? The people here, like you, are all at the mercy of the Sheikh. He has made himself a small empire with powerful investors. He must be providing the super-rich with something unattainable from the outside world."

Charlotte swallowed.

"He is giving them complete freedom to do whatever they want with absolute privacy from the eyes of the outside world."

Charlotte felt the full realisation of that statement wash through her. "What do they want?"

"With no moral barriers? I absolutely dread to think."

Chapter 18

The absence of Mother Pascal marked a clear change in the morning's hymn practice. The new choirmaster, a short, rounded man usually hiding in the wings, had risen to the challenge, directing his choir to sing hymn after hymn without interruption or correction. Charlotte relaxed into the familiar words and tunes, allowing her mind to wander over her conversation with the Prime Minister's wife.

Bernadine seemed quieter than usual. Perhaps she disliked the shameless bingeing of music. It seemed callous that the new choirmaster was protesting against Pascal's studious methods of music study. The celebratory purge of music seemed to darken her mood with every new choral piece.

"I thought singing was a definite no-no in a strict Islamic set up," Jasmine whispered to Charlotte.

"Maybe Mr Stramford requested all these hymns for his funeral? I'm not complaining."

"It's not a funeral. It's a service of remembrance... you know, no body." "Thanks for the clarification!" Charlotte said, resisting the impulse to laugh.

Bernadine stole a glance at the two before looking down at her feet. The women were all dressed in their grey tunics, though the headscarves were for the most part, pulled down.

With the service due to start that very afternoon, there was a tangible excitement in the choir stalls. The change of leadership was fresh news and with the tablets issued almost immediately, many of the Abbey inhabitants felt gagged as it was no secret that those small computers were very efficient listening devices.

Pat, late from her night shift with Michael, quickened her pace towards the voices of the choir, she loved singing even though her voice was beaten from all the smoking. Taking a faster route across the graveyard and reaching the old monks' cells, she broke into a trot, feeling the ancient stone slabs smooth against her sandals. Then, for no obvious reason at all, Pat felt a great pull of melancholy about her midriff, so severe that it slowed her to a walk, then a standstill. She rested her hand against the wall of the first of the monks' cells. What was this? What was this?

A strange tingling played upon her fingers, followed by a noticeable weakening of her limbs. Her body felt heavy. Was she having a stroke? She had heard of this. What was the test? Can she smile? Does one side of her mouth pull down? No mirror, can't do that one. Can she lift both arms? Yes, she could. There was nothing wrong with her body other than a strange fatigue which seemed to stem from this inexplicable sadness. Why was she feeling like this? So sudden, so strange. Perhaps this was a sign Michael had died, she had heard of people experiencing premonitions, and perhaps this was one. The best thing seemed to be to just... lower herself down... just here at the doorway of this monks' cell. She felt little shrubs peeking out between the old stonework. The tablet began to vibrate from within her tunic. She ignored it and used all her strength to lower herself right to a stoney, grassy mound. From a seated position, she felt better. There was no panic, just a calm sort of melancholy. She focused on the scent of the disturbed earth, the grass between her fingers. Finally, the tablet ceased its vibrations and a distinct but very quiet knocking met her ears. Knock, knock... knock, knock... Then a pause, as if the knocker was gathering strength, then again knock, knock... knock, knock.

Pat strained her ears. Where was it coming from? The old cells were empty, surely?

A clatter of footsteps quickly approached and within no time Mr Wilks and two men she did not recognise appeared.

"Pat? Are you unwell?"

Pat looked at the small group but could not muster the energy to respond.

"Send for the medics. Can you hear me, Pat?"

"Yeah, I can 'ear yu."

The choirmaster leapt up from the piano, offering encouraging words to the choir about their notable improvement over the past year and how honoured Mr Stramford would be to have the glorious Stramford Abbey voices sing his favourite hymns for his memorial service. Charlotte listened but struggled to focus. Mrs Nkosi had confided her deepest fears to her, though she hardly knew the woman. Why? This information entrusted to her could have potentially dangerous consequences if mismanaged. Another thought that rose unbidden was that though this choir practice was a good two hours long, Pat had uncharacteristically failed to show up. Charlotte knew that Pat adored singing and would happily leap out of bed in the early hours of a frosty morning if it meant choir practice; furthermore, she had said to Charlotte she would be here just last night as she headed out to her night shift with Michael. So where was she?

Charlotte looked at Jasmine, who was looking right back at her. She motioned at Bernadine with her eyes, the poor thing looked miserable.

The choirmaster wittered on, clearly enjoying the elevated status of his new position. Charlotte actively blocked him out and stared at her shoes, it allowed her to think. Mother Pascal has disappeared and Bernadine appears devastated at the loss. Is this because she was a shepherd figure to little Bernadine? Charlotte glanced toward the small figure, somehow alone amongst the other choir members. She certainly looked like a lamb ready for slaughter. Another thought... where does Pat fit into all this? She was no fan of Pascal, and the feeling was certainly mutual. Are they locked in a padded cell together? Or worse... dead? No, that was stupid.

Finally released, Charlotte broke into a fast trot across the graveyard. Jasmine hung back with Bernadine, though they were catching up. There were just a few hours until the memorial service. Charlotte's worries bubbled in her stomach as she fast walked. Scanning around her, everything seemed as it should be, the old gravestones motionless against the sharp Autumnal breeze. A collection of brown leaves scraped across the path in swirls. A very light drizzle started, and Charlotte felt the tiny droplets play in her eyelashes. Looking back, she saw her two friends and a cluster of others heading after her. 'Swallow it down,' Charlotte told herself. Intuition is all very well, but without strong evidence, it is plain dangerous to dabble in the unknown. Mrs Nkosi's suspicions remained theoretical unless proven to be correct.

Michael remained alive, though by a thread. The doctor administered strong sedatives at the request of Michael's parents. The other Praise group patients took part in their daily activities, art, baking, and the ever-popular PlayStation. Jasmine worked with Tilly and two other residents. According to her tablet, Charlotte was on housemaid duties this morning, changing the bed linen for the Praise group residents. Usually, this would be shared with two or even three people as it made the job easier, but Charlotte found herself alone. The rooms led off down a corridor, Michael's the first and the rest leading back from there. The trolley had to be collected from the laundry room and wheeled down the corridor as the residents took part in their activities. Why was she alone? Heading to the recreation room, she saw with surprise, Mr Wilks standing by the coffee machine helping himself. This seemed to strike pure terror in Bernadine, who shrank from the kitchen and bolted straight for the art corner. Noting her friend's behaviour, she walked into the kitchen.

"Excuse me sir, but I appear to be alone on housekeeping."

He turned and fixed his eyes on hers. Charlotte was having none of it. He may have scared Bernadine half to death, but he caused no fear in her. Looking at the full coffee pot and considering whether it would be bad form to ask for a cup, she said,

"The bedlinen has to be done in pairs. I'm usually with Pat." She coolly returned his gaze.

"Where is she anyway?"

He took a long pause to sip his coffee.

"Unfortunately, Patricia has taken ill and is resting in the infirmary."

"What sort of ill?" Charlotte barked a little too quickly.

"Patient confidentiality does not allow me to share that information with you. It would seem now that you have a lot to do in a rather short space of time." Cradling his coffee, he moved away.

Charlotte had visions of pummelling his arrogant face with the rolled-up towels she still carried. Opting for a stolen coffee instead, she returned to the laundry trolley, towels intact, coffee steaming in her hand. An impossible hour stretched before her. Replacing all the sheets took much longer than it should have. With two workers, the sheets would glide on effortlessly with a few well-placed tucks. Now Charlotte was forced to go from side-to-side tucking and retucking as she noticed with dismay that it was nearly impossible to judge whether the sheet was symmetrical until it was too late. This resulted in her having to rip it off and start again. By the fifth room, Charlotte had improved her technique and with a well-formed flap, could place the large sheets effectively the first time around.

It was only when she stooped to tuck the final corner that she heard the door softly closing behind her.

She immediately tensed. Before she could gather herself to swing around, two strong arms pulled around her shoulders, forcing her elbows uselessly by her sides. In a flash, her face was thrust half under the arm of her assailant as a strong scent of expensive cologne hit her nostrils. She twisted her head out of the underarm vice scratching her cheek painfully on something sharp, a zip? A button? She began to scream, a fear-fuelled eruption from her lungs. An almighty push sent her reeling. The scream was quashed and replaced with a gargle of bloody saliva. Finding herself on the floor, she could see her attacker. Mr Wilks stood half panting like a carnal creature starved out of its mind, and oh so horribly, Charlotte knew it was her that he wished to feast upon.

She placed her hand on her throbbing face. All that strength she had felt just a short while ago by the coffee machine ebbed wretchedly away as she desperately tried to think what to do. Maybe she could pacify him? He wouldn't risk seriously hurting her, would he? She remembered Bernadine's face. Oh God.

"I have you at last." His eyes were glassy.

Charlotte felt a wave of revulsion, her vulnerability was turning him on.

In a sudden movement, he was on top of her, his hands pinning her shoulders back,

Charlotte screamed again, but this time, a hand released her shoulder and clamped across her mouth. The hand tasted salty. Too flat to bite. The shoulder release allowed her to throw her full weight into a roll which unbalanced him, allowing for a moment of freedom. Charlotte launched herself at the door, pulling at the handle with all her strength. A terrible realisation swam over her. He'd locked it.

With a sob of frustration, she turned to look at him. He still wore that crazed needy expression, though he seemed calmer, like a cat who had cornered a mouse. He seemed to be enjoying the chase. Cocking his head to one side, he began a smile that did not reach his eyes. Some time passed; his expression changed. Was he listening to something out in the corridor?

Charlotte craned her ears to hear. Was someone there?

"If you so much as squeak, little mouse, I will hurt you very badly," he hissed.

Charlotte nodded obediently, hating her cowardice. Was there some sort of weapon she could use to overpower him? The water jug, perhaps? The bedpan?

He was still listening. He took out his tablet and looked closely at the location plan, looking at the moving dots, determining who was outside. His brow furrowed as he replaced the tablet. His eyes returned to Charlotte.

Voices from behind the door were getting louder. A deep mumble punctuated by a woman's voice, clearly distressed as her wailing and sobbing crescendoed. The effect on Mr Wilks was astonishing. Aggressively throwing Charlotte to one side, he quickly unlocked the door and slipped out into the approaching commotion.

Charlotte took a few moments. That was too close. She looked at her hands, they were shaking. Her heart was thumping furiously against her chest. She needed to get away, she needed to make sense of what had just happened. The screaming was getting louder and more terrified right outside the door.

With her still shaking hands, she twisted the handle and the door fell open. A great commotion poured into the room and around her. Mrs Nkosi was being manhandled by her husband and Mr Compton as tears streamed down her face.

"Please, leave me be! Let me alone! I will not be treated this way! I will not! Animals! Absolute animals!"

Finally, as if Bim Nkosi had been delaying until this very minute, he put his strong arms around his wife, silencing her screams into his chest. The two stood in the centre of the room in an uncomfortable waltz. Mrs Nkosi, tiny in comparison to her dance partner. "It's ok, it's all over now, it's all over now," he mumbled over and over, quieter and quieter, until his eyes left hers and met those of Mr Compton, who took a single vial and injected its contents into Mrs Nkosi's arm.

She could not move much; just her eyes flicked up to her husband.

"How could you?" They seemed to say, though within moments, they flickered and closed.

"You'll be ok, love, you'll be ok."

Effortlessly, he lifted his wife into his arms and began to leave the room. Charlotte desperately tried to catch her father's eye but couldn't as he moved straight to the Prime Minister to guide him forward. Mr Wilks and two other men Charlotte only slightly recognised talked in hushed tones, though she heard snippets.

"Because the boy died... some sort of fit... convulsions... she should have left the room... who knows what they'll do? It's like they're alive in that state..." The voices trailed out of earshot.

Charlotte slumped down to the floor and hugged her knees.

Chapter 19

Down the corridor, she ran through the kitchen area and into the now empty recreation room. She stopped. It looked chaotic, though eerily silent. Books and craft materials were scattered about the tables, paint brushes unrinsed and hardening. The usual meticulous clean-up had obviously been abandoned, perhaps in a hasty retreat as the distressed Mrs Nkosi approached. Were all the residents at the memorial service, too? Surely not. Charlotte's tablet buzzed with a reminder. Memorial service 7 minutes. She took some slow breaths, anxious to slow the unrelenting adrenaline coursing around her. She needed time.

6 minutes

The silence broke with the sound of a quiet vibration, not her device. It was coming from the corner of the room; there, sitting on the top of the books, was a tablet. Charlotte quickly went over and picked it up. She swiped the screen. 'Welcome Compton, ' it read. For a moment, Charlotte was startled to see her surname but then immediately realised it must be her father's tablet. Why was it here? Maybe he'd just plonked the thing down when he was racing after Mrs Nkosi with his sedative. Charlotte's thoughts whipped back to her childhood. He was inclined to lose things, keys, glasses, tv remote. She smiled at the memory of her father scouring the house for his glasses, only to discover them on his forehead. Could this then just be a clumsy mistake?

5 minutes

Oh God. Quickly, she swiped the screen again. 'Welcome Compton' it repeated. She swiped. It opened. It actually opened. 'No password, dad?' she grinned to herself. He must not have set it up yet. This was just too easy. Quickly, she opened the location app. Where was everybody? She zoomed in. She could see the small group of men with Mr Wilks moving closer to the Abbey where the memorial service was to take place. Nearly every dot was amalgamated into a huge blob, taking up nearly all the Abbey's ground space, but where was she? Ah, there she was, with her father in the recreation room. Surely he would get into trouble for this? Someone would notice.

Charlotte's tablet never gave away the location of any of the leadership figures of the Abbey, but Mr Compton's certainly did. All dots were initialled

and therefore mostly meaningless to her, save HP, Heather Pascal. It had to be. There she was, a lonely dot in the monks' cells.

4 minutes.

Oh God, she would have to run. Quickly erasing the tablet's search history, she put it on standby and went out the double doors across the graveyard, where she could see a large crowd around the Abbey. She was running late, but she was not actually late yet.

Her jog turned to a sprint and oh relief! in the line of women in headscarves, one turned exposing a frond of Afro hair and a beautiful profile, so recognisable. Their eyes met and in a moment, Charlotte was with Jasmine.

"Put up your headscarf for God's sake!" She hissed.

"What the hell has happened to you? You're bleeding?!"

"Wilks, bloody Wilks had a go."

"Oh God" Jasmine risked a turn. "You're shaking. Oh Charlotte, you're alright?"

A cascade of bells rang across the grounds as the crowd began to file into the Abbey.

"Jasmine, I need your help."

"What?"

Charlotte risked nearly shouting over the bells,

"I need you to cover for me!"

"How? What are you talking about?"

Charlotte put her mouth close to Jasmine's ear and relayed what she could before discreetly handing her tablet to her friend.

"When we get to that holly bush there. I'm going to jump behind it. We're at the back. No one should see unless they turn."

"That's bloody risky," Jasmine retorted.

"I'll be back by the holly when you get out. Just make sure you stand there, and I'll get my tablet back off you."

The bells paused and the two women fell silent. Jasmine looked fearfully at her friend but said no more. They arrived at the bush. Heart thumping, Charlotte quickly ducked behind it. The dark grey tunic and headscarf was a blessing in that it camouflaged her well against the dark foliage. With the last man in, the great door thumped shut.

A great feeling of liberation took hold of her. She had two glorious hours free of the tracking device. Freedom to find out what was going on here. She felt physical pain when she thought of Mrs Nkosi but had no clue where they had taken her. The only lead she had was Mother Pascal and though Charlotte thoroughly disliked the woman, she suspected she was the key to unlocking many truths about Stramford Abbey.

Hastily, she darted to the hedge line and thankful for the drizzle that now blew about, made her way to the monks' cells. There were many bushes to cover her as it bordered the graveyard. Right on the perimeter and in plain sight of the monks' cells stood a huge headstone at an impressive 45-

degree angle. She crouched under it feeling like a little girl hiding in the park after dusk, rebellious and naughty.

The drizzle amalgamated on the headstone to form larger drops. Charlotte watched them, hypnotised. They'd enlarge until wobbling precariously, finally letting go and falling to a satisfying splat.

Fearful thoughts began to crowd into her head. Why had she taken this enormous risk, leaving the full cohort to spy upon secrets she had no means to influence. With a frustrated sigh, she pulled herself out from under the stone. Standing in the rain felt good.

Checking all about her, she pulled up her headscarf and made her way over to the monks' cells. This is where Pascal's solitary dot had flashed on the tablet device. She looked carefully at the entrance where once a wooden door would have hung, but now it gaped open to a dark cell of ancient stones peppered with tiny succulents and wispy yellow grasses. There were six in total, ranging from near ruins to the one she stood at now, which, save the missing door, was intact. She had never been inside before. She ducked in the low doorway and took a moment to allow her eyes to adjust. It was a small space with an earthy floor. An old wooden pew had been left against the back wall.

She cleared her throat. Fighting the urge to sing, she opted to whistle instead, rather tuneless but as the pitch got lower, she felt the satisfying reverberations of the tiny cell. She sang out a hymn line slowly, deliberately pausing to hear the echo.

She stopped, twisting her head to the side. Had she heard something? A scratching sound. It stopped, and then a tapping began. Where was it coming from? Charlotte crouched down in the earth and gently, on all fours followed the sound. It led behind the old pew, right into the corner. There was a tuft of some kind of plant she didn't recognise. Spurred on by the sound she grabbed one side of the pew and tried to heave it away, but it was so heavy, she could only just move it about a metre. Stepping into the newly exposed gap, she put her hand to the tufty plant. It seemed to be emitting a jet of cool air. Puzzled, Charlotte started to explore, pulling away at the plant and revealing some sort of small cast iron vent. She put her ear down to the small grate. There were sounds of movement, clothes rustling or half muted footfalls.

Her head was so close to the ground that she could almost chew the earthy scent of the freshly pulled plant.

"Hello?" She whispered tentatively.

She waited. The distant clock struck half past the hour. Only an hour and a half left.

Footfalls.

She tensed. There were at least two people outside in the rain. Stiffening against the wall she continued to listen.

There were voices, a few male and one female. They seemed in high spirits.

Charlotte began to shiver. The stone wall was impossibly cold. Pulling away from it, she gently climbed over the pew and stood right at the entrance, hidden in the shadows. Gently craning her neck, she risked a quick glimpse. The Sheikh, the chief of security, who was that woman in the headscarf? And a third taller man. Was it Mr Nkosi? He was certainly broad like him. The misty rain and the distance made it hard to be sure.

A tiny scream from the vent hit her ears. That was a scream, wasn't it? Swiftly and silently, she vaulted back over the pew. Taking up her old position, she lowered her ear to the iron grate.

Chapter 20

The Sheikh's exclusive whisky collection down in the old crypt had a healing effect on Bim who, still stunned from the events of the last hour, needed the reassuring burn of Macallan's premier 15-year-old whisky down his throat. Pauline, safely away in the hospital wing, could give him no more heartache as she lay sedated under the watchful eye of the doctors. What had happened in that room was both a relief and a nightmare. The boy's bizarre burst of life just as the euthanasia was administered had all but destroyed Pauline. It was all over now, though. A slow healing needed to start, Pauline by his side, the way things were.

"Come," smiled the Sheikh,

"I have much to show you while the ceremony is in motion."

Slightly staggering after the Sheikh, Bim started in surprise to see what appeared to be Heather Pascal suddenly there in the crypt wine cellar with them. She stood as still as a mannequin, looking down at him from the top of the stairs.

"Mr Nkosi sir, I'm so sorry for your loss." She began to descend the steps holding on to the metal bannister yet not taking her eyes away from him.

"Michael was a fine young man, God rest his soul. I'm disappointed that I could not be with you when dearest

Pauline needed me most, but I assure you I'm intent on making up for my absence in the months to come."

Bim smiled at her with uncertainty. She seemed rather different, though he could not put a finger on why.

"Heather, it's good to see you. I know Pauline is really rather desperate to see you. You've been unwell. I was sorry to hear that."

"Only a bad bout of influenza, though I'm happy to say I'm back to full strength now. May I join you, gentlemen?"

"Yes, yes, come with us," came the husky voice of the Sheikh, coughing to clear his throat.

The three moved up out of the crypt wine cellar and swiftly through the Abbey grounds, eventually stopping by the monks' cells. Dark clouds rolled in ominously, threatening downpours. As the first large raindrops fell, they

were met by James, chief of security. He nodded respectfully to the small party and looked inquisitively to the Sheikh as if awaiting instruction.

The Sheikh gave a short affirmative nod to James who, using his device, initialised a mechanical shuddering about them. Bim almost shouted out in shock as the ground shook violently enough to cause them all to adjust their stance. Right in front of the small party, a great grassy tile slid up and to the side, revealing a beautiful marble set of stairs descending out of view. They were illuminated with subtle lighting concealed within the bannisters.

"Well, who'd have thought it? It's like Aladdin's ruddy cave!" Smiled Bim in amazement.

The Sheikh nodded respectfully, motioning the Prime minister to go first. The small group made their descent down the spectacular stairway, wide yet shallow steps winding round to the right and finally ending in a large circular room. There were a number of glass doorways evenly placed around the walls.

"Welcome to the greatest laboratory in the world, dear friend. It is referred to as the Research Centre, though it is not in the common knowledge."

The Sheikh beamed unreservedly.

"This has the greatest scientists. Here they are staying Mr Nkosi, working on the most, the greatest projects the world has ever seen."

Bim broke away from the party and ran his hands along the bevelled wood that separated the glass doors. He had never seen anything like it.

"This really is exceptional, Sir."

"Come, come, my friend, there is much to discuss." He beckoned the prime minister to join him in one of the rooms.

"Heather, you are coming too, yes?"

"Of course," she nodded.

The three entered a rather sparse meeting room with a large glass table in the middle and office chairs surrounding it. They took seats while The Sheikh turned on a large flat-screened monitor attached to the wall. It blinked awake, showing a beautiful mountain range screensaver. James tapped something into his tablet for a few moments, then walked out and back up the stairs. Before following the others into the room, Bim took a good look at the remaining doors and saw with surprise that some seemed to lead not into rooms but corridors with doors branching off those.

"How big is this place?" he said to Pascal.

"The Research complex was created by Mr Stramford sir, many years ago. It was built to enable scientific research into cutting edge treatments for cancers, mainly of the lungs, breast and prostate... latterly much progress was made with leukaemia. But not only that, but huge funding went into research into pain relief treatments to increase their effectiveness across all manner of ailments whilst reducing the more destructive side effects."

"That's incredible. But why here? Why is it hidden like this?"

"The research here has grown exponentially mainly because all the usual legal constraints have been lifted."

"What sort of constraints? Ethical ones, you mean?"

The Sheikh, who had been listening intently, intervened.

"This western habit you are having, to insure, to safeguard. It is causing problem all the time. All the time. We are not going to find cure if we cannot test our hypothesis. Is that not right, Mr Prime Minister? We are needing some peace from the western lawyers to take the... ah... issues... and fixing it."

"So this research is a... a... clandestine operation?"

"I am not knowing this word. This operation, so you are calling it, is a breakthrough for the future of humanity."

Removing his glasses to polish them, the Sheikh pulled out the chair with his free hand.

"I am showing you this, Mr Prime Minister because you are investing much interest in this place, and I am seeing you can give much heart to the continuation of such a project. You may need the... researching for your own matters too sir, if I can explain."

Bim felt a twinge in his neck, the start of a muscular strain, perhaps. Maybe he had been tensing without realising. There was a lot to get his head around on such a traumatic day anyway. It was strange to have started the day happily eating croissants with his wife and cajoling the cat to end it here, in this peculiar underground labyrinth, slightly tipsy from the Macallan and increasingly perplexed by the unashamed excitement in the eyes of this most powerful Sheikh from Saudi Arabia sitting across from him.

"I'm sorry Sheikh Mohamed, it's been quite a day. I'm sorry if I'm not entirely following you."

The Sheikh patted Bim about the shoulder blades with obvious affection.

"It is better if the... you are saying, elegant? Eloquent? Mother Pascal explaining to you and I am listening. I have photos here," he pointed to the large screen.

"If I link my phone... yes it is screen sharing. Here, yes."

The screen flashed quickly through his gallery photos at such a speed that Bim took his eyes away quite nauseated.

"You have been invited by dear Sheikh Mohamed Imran to share in the wonder of the most groundbreaking scientific success in history. It cannot be shared outside these walls because it is currently frowned upon in universal law. However, from the most progressive and entrepreneurial minds in society, I am now able to share with you the results of the biggest scientific breakthrough ever made in living history."

Mother Pascal's voice quivered slightly like a child about to reveal her A+ report card to her parents.

Bim shifted uncomfortably. Were they waiting for him to burst into happy tears? If this science was so damn progressive, why was he not facing a panel of top scientists in a cutting-edge laboratory or conference room? The twinge in his neck nagged uncomfortably.

A still image appeared on the screen. It showed scientists working in a lab, and there were close-ups of what they were working on. A human ear could be seen in a petri dish. Mice ran around a cage and as the camera zoomed in, Bim could see each one had a long human finger growing where the tail should be. His stomach turned, and the twinge in his neck travelled through his shoulder. A large animal, what was it? A pig. A pig lay unconscious on an operating table, linked up to breathing tubes and drips. It was alive, Bim saw its chest rise and fall. Several people in lab coats appeared to take samples from the pig and place them under the magnifying glass. What were they looking for? What were they doing?

"I... I am not good with medical things, I'm afraid. Perhaps you could explain what you have discovered instead?" Bim grimaced.

Mother Pascal smiled with understanding. "Do you remember, years back, scientists managed to clone a sheep. It was an identical replica of its mother."

"Yes, yes, I remember that. Dolly the Sheep, wasn't it? Yes, I remember."

"What if I were to tell you that we have managed to clone the first human. A genetically identical match, just as Dolly was."

206

Mother Pascal afforded a quick glimpse over to Sheikh Mohamed Imran, who sat back in his chair, hands resting across his large abdomen.

"You've cloned a human? You've made... a twin?" Bim felt his head lightening. This was the stuff of sci-fi. American films where the armies of cloned psychopaths destroy everything in their wake like locusts. Something in Bim broke. This was wrong. This was so wrong.

"You can't... you just can't do that!" he stammered.

"We have doing that already!" laughed the Sheikh, again fatherly clapping his hands across Bim's shoulders. "It is magnificent, no?"

Bim swallowed. His throat sandpapery

"I'm afraid this may be wholly unethical. Cancer treatment is one thing; experimental genetic engineering is quite another."

"Come come, Prime Minister. It is a momentous discovery. You will see how it is a wonderful thing. Of course, I am understanding in bad hands this is most terrible.

"Catastrophic," Bim murmured.

Appearing not to notice, the Sheikh continued.

"But in our hands sir, I see great progress for the collective future... of humanity, inshallah."

"Our hands?!"

Mother Pascal interjected,

"Mr Nkosi, you understand how Mr Stramford set this institution up as a way of insuring all humanity could receive the care and love they needed in a safe environment away from the dangers of the outside world. They were offered entertainment, spiritual healing, sports and activities right up until the day they died, like, God rest his soul, dear Michael."

"Yes, of course."

"What if Sheikh Mohamed Imran has progressed on from that very same mantra, offering, for an appropriate price of course, the opportunity for people who have suffered misfortune in their lives to be healed and start afresh.

"Healed and start afresh? I'm not following."

Suddenly, as if the Sheikh had experienced enough, he kicked out at a chair, nearly toppling it over.

"Come, Mr Prime Minister, this talking is not helping. Come, I will show you. Come."

He extended out his hand towards the door and motioned Bim to follow.

Glad to get out of the conference room, Bim obliged. They took a glass door and went down a corridor. Taking the second door on the right, they entered another corridor, then took an elevator down to a great open laboratory. It was huge, with a series of vents circulating fresh air down to the dozen or so scientists who moved about purposefully. There were huge freezers and rows and rows of cupboards, microscopes, large robotic machines, which operated autonomously, sorting through selections of frozen vials and placing them back in industrial sized ice boxes. Bizarrely, a crate of small goats stood in the middle of the room. They cried out periodically, but were largely ignored by both scientists and Bim's companions. Bim couldn't stand the noise. It cut through him like the wail of an infant.

Clearing his throat to protest, he realised his companions had walked out of earshot and were stationary at a large steel door with a security system flashing red. Bim, discarding his complaint, caught back up with them. The Sheikh placed his thumb on the pad and the lights turned green. In a moment, the heavy door slid to the side, revealing a small domestic looking room. Even though the walls were made of thick glass, the interior was covered in soft furnishings. A small sofa and upholstered chair, a rug, a bookcase. A portable electric heater and two paintings of Jesus, one with his crown of thorns and his eyes cast skyward. A small, presumably bathroom took up a corner with a drape for modesty.

"Heather?" the Sheikh said.

"I'll be with you now." A voice came from within the bathroom.

Bim furrowed his brow and looked at Heather Pascal by his side, who, rather oddly, was looking straight at him as if waiting for his reaction.

"Er... who?" Bim looked sideways at the curtain, then back at Heather. "Who's in there?" He whispered, feeling his hands begin to sweat.

Chapter 21

There were definitely voices down there. Charlotte could hear them, but only just. The bells from the Abbey had been tolling throughout the afternoon and the rain had made a pleasantly percussive soundscape, but now, now she needed silence. She needed to hear what those tiny voices were saying.

A shuddering intruded on her frustrations as the great grass tile slid open again. The first time had seemed like an earth tremor and instinctively taking cover, she had been amazed to see a security officer descending into the ground.

This time though, Charlotte was ready, she leapt over the pew and took her place at the cell wall. She couldn't hear any voices, but surely someone must have entered or indeed exited the strange gateway. Risking a glance, she popped her head around the monks' cell wall. She froze. There in the distance, stood the chief of security, looking straight at her. A prickle of panic shot down her spine. She stayed frozen, willing him to turn away. A second passed, then as if he'd heard her prayers, he proceeded to sweep his gaze across the whole perimeter of the graveyard and then turning his back did the same to the opposite side. The tile shuddered into place. Surely he hadn't noticed half a small face peering out of the monk's cell. No need to panic... no quick movements... Charlotte carefully moved her head out of sight and back into the reassuring darkness. That was close. She cursed her stupidity. 'Why didn't I just go right on out there and dance?!' She dug her nails into her palms. 'Bloody idiot.'

Feeling slightly giddy from the near miss, she more cautiously took up her place at her listening station. There were no bells, the rain had stopped. Nothing.

Placing her right ear right to the small vent she strained to hear.

"Do you…. years back. Scientists managed to clone… It was an identical replica of…"

Charlotte's brow furrowed. The tiny female voice was familiar, but she couldn't place it.

"Yes, yes, I remember that. Dolly the Sheep, wasn't it? Yes, I remember."

This voice was easier to hear, deeper, recognisable. The Prime Minister. It must be. He was in the Praise group rooms only half an hour ago, wrestling with his distraught wife. What was he doing down there?

"I were to tell you… managed to clone the first human. A genetically identical match, just as…"

Charlotte held her breath, straining to hear more.

"Cloned a human? You've made… a twin?… genetically identical…"

What the hell was going on down there? Were Mrs Nkosi's fears true then? Cloning humans. Had someone been cloned already? Oh God, this was big.

"You can't... you just can't do that!"

Charlotte pulled herself away from the vent and sat very still. The juxtaposition of the miraculous discovery to the sinister implications all churning away deep under the ground. A clone couldn't possibly be the same person, only a physical copy. They're able to clone people. They're able to clone people.' Charlotte repeated the sentence to herself several times, yet it had no meaning. Would the clone be grown in a test tube and progress through the ages and stages of a natural life or were they instant true to age replicas? If so, how would cognitive function or memory work?

She forced herself to listen to the drips of rain at the entrance to get back into the present. Her cheek throbbed lightly, the ghost of Mr Wilk's zip imprinted in her cheek.

What was she to do with this information? Her body began to tremble. Was it fear or the cold? She felt vulnerable and useless in the plastic sandals and thin black tunic, her feeble protection against the sharp gusts that entered the stone cell. What time was it? Hugging her knees tighter, she realised with dismay that she had no means to measure the passing time. Her device was safely stowed away in Jasmine's tunic.

Bach's 'Jesu of Man's Desiring' was coming to an end, and the full voice of the choir filled the Abbey. Flames from numerous candles danced as if affected by the optimism of the melody. The choir's voices lifted, crescendoing with hope and compassion for one man who lay cold, awaiting heaven.

Jasmine felt tired from all the standing and the extra tablet device weighed heavily in her tunic pocket as well as her conscience. As the second hour reached its end, she swallowed uncomfortably, her voice slightly hoarse from all the singing.

She looked to her left and saw Bernadine, who appeared to sway fractionally from side to side. She looked weak and small, more so than she ever had before. Jasmine allowed her fingers to trace the corners of Charlotte's tablet device like she was concealing a knife. Had she become just too reckless this time?

The lights dimmed and a two-minute silence was instigated by a lonely trumpet fanfare, its bright sound echoing between the high ceiling and stone walls. The dancing flames slowed to a waltz. The congregation bowed their heads respectfully.

Bernadine felt slightly giddy as she had not eaten for hours. Her thoughts wandered as the trumpet signalled the end of the silence. The great Edward Stramford had so selflessly strived all his life for this huge Christian community that had flourished in the Abbey. Bernadine looked nervously at the rows of heads and felt acutely that Stramford's loss had created a tangible fear within the Abbey's walls. She tried to think of some words of comfort from the Bible. How could Mr Stramford's strong ethos of care and Christian compassion continue with the Sheikh? She felt his wandering hands and could smell his spiced cologne. Shuddering, she tried to pull her thoughts back to the service, her companions, the holy space.

James paced back and forth several times before checking his tablet again. Mr Nkosi's return was imminent and both he and the Sheikh would need to be taken over to the Abbey for the final half hour of the remembrance service. Sharp gusts of wind lifted autumnal leaves into tall twisters before dispersing them about the grass to begin the cycle again. Attempting to take in the expansive Abbey grounds, he looked out to the oak trees and then back across towards the Abbey. The monks' cells stuck oddly from the grass, some crumbling, others sturdy.

A fine misty rain had started up, it travelled in oscillations as strong gusts took hold. The rain became thicker, large splodges hit his leather shoes, leaving Matisse like stains. Pulling up his hood he jogged and then ran over to the monks' cells. He needed shelter. Ducking to clear the low ceiling, he stepped inside. Immediate movement startled him, yet his eyes could not adjust to the gloom. Squinting at the far corner of the cell, he tensed.

There was a shuffle of cloth and suddenly, a figure flew beside him ducking down by his waist. James' arm shot out and easily caught the shoulder of what could only have been a very frightened young woman. She gasped and began clawing at his hand to release her.

"Hey up hey up steady on. You're ok, it's ok. Just slow down."

The struggle stopped but the woman shook as if consumed by cold or fear.

"I'm not going to hurt you, you just surprised me." "I need to go."

James looked hard at the woman. She looked familiar. Her headscarf had come away and her hair was in disarray over her shoulders. Something about her face struck a chord, but he couldn't place it.

"I cannot let you go until you tell me who you are and what you're doing here."

Charlotte did not answer.

He stood authoritatively but not aggressively in front of the entrance blocking her in. He seemed irritated, not at her but at the situation.

"Are you carrying anything?"

"No."

"You're one of the red shirts here, are you?"

Charlotte sensed something like kindness about the uniformed man but stayed silent. Finally, after some time in a smaller voice she said.

"Let me go."

He looked slightly anguished, "God's sake," he clicked his tongue in frustration, then looked at her again.

"What are your intentions? Why are you not at the service?" "Just let me go."

James let out a small, irritated whistle.

"Look, I need to know why and how you're here." He looked briefly at his watch.

"I don't want to turn you in. You know as well as I do that you would face serious consequences... Why are you here? Have you run away?"

He didn't wait for an answer. Pulling out his tablet, he flicked it on and began opening and closing apps and squinting at the screen as he read. Looking from his tablet to Charlotte a few times, his expression softened.

"You're Compton's daughter, aren't you?"

Charlotte tried to conceal her thumping heart. How did this security officer know how to find that out? Were they already actively looking for her?

"I need to go," she repeated weakly.

"Thought I recognised your face..." He looked at his watch again.

"Look, I'm probably going to hang for this, but listen up. I know your father well. He is an outstanding man. I should take you to the Stramford room right now so you face a hearing. Looking at your record here so far, you will not be given a fair trial and instead carted off to the Abbey jail... which I... which..." he tailed off and looked over Charlotte's shoulder at the corner she had sheltered in. "I couldn't let that happen to Compton's kid."

Charlotte studied him. He looked torn, yet he stood resolute, too. Could she break away and just get far enough away that he would give up the chase? She studied him, there was no hostility there... then she could race back the hill to the holly bush and wait for Jasmine. The security guard seemed to be wrestling with his conscience. The hold on her shoulder kept wavering, then tightening again. She could tell he was in a predicament. Had he been Wilks, who knows what horrors could have befallen her, but this man seemed to have integrity.

He took her forearm gently but without room for manoeuvre. Allowing herself to be led outside the cave, Charlotte felt a thin film of rain across her face.

"Will you let me go back? Can't I just run back to the service? I managed to escape, but I'm ready to go back now.

Please?" She looked at him with such intense emotion that she could see the immediate effect on his face.

"You must swear to me though, swear that you will not repeat this careless behaviour. I don't think your father could take the consequences and the repercussions would be catastrophic."

He looked at the closed entrance to the Research Centre, then back at Charlotte.

"I'm soon to appear over there with people who could take you straight into hell. Do you understand what I mean by hell?"

Charlotte nodded.

"If I can see you, even as a dot on the horizon, the game is up."

With that, he released her arm, turned his back and walked purposefully to the hidden entrance. Charlotte bolted at full speed away from the monks' cells, away from him and headed for the cover of the hedgerows. Something in her heart felt light as if her miraculous escape was due to some divine intervention. Perhaps that security officer with the kind eyes had been sent by God to keep her safe. Her shivers ebbed away as the run warmed her through.

Chapter 22

Pat woke suddenly in a strange bed, in a strange room, with noticeably strange lighting. It was electrical and harsh yet weirdly dim at the same time. She immediately felt for her St. Christopher necklace that she always wore and found it with some relief. Her fingers caressed the warm coin.

Turning her head to the side, she could see a hospital table with a plastic water jug, beaker and a bell. A heart monitor was behind it but switched off. Above her bed, save the odd lighting, boasted a new looking suspended ceiling. The walls were white, one single door was visible but shut. There was no window.

Pat supposed she should ring the bell but opted instead to take a moment to try to recollect how she got there. It was hard, she couldn't remember anything at all.

Unnerved, she put both hands to St. Christopher again. Right, so she had been on her way to choir, she had passed the Monks' cells and... Oh no... she hadn't passed them at all. She had fainted or had she collapsed? It was peculiar, what *had* happened?

Taking her hands from her necklace, she began a tentative exploration. Could she wriggle her toes? Were her knees intact? Her elbows, her wrists?

Ok, so she was in one piece that was something, but the complete blank scared her. What had happened in that time? She reached up to her hair. It seemed unnaturally soft as if newly washed, her nails were clean and even her usually yellow nicotine-stained fingers appeared revitalised, as if somehow, while unconscious she had been treated at some exclusive spa.

But why?

An unpleasant thought began to surface. Why had someone gone to so much trouble to 'clean' her? What had happened to her that required cleaning? Was something untoward being covered up?

"Oh whatever, ye daft shite," She said out loud to herself.

Her voice seemed muffled and unnatural. One side of her throat felt sore.

Had there been a tube inserted down there? All at once, Pat felt fearful.

"Hello?" She called.

"Hello?" She called out again, trying to sit up.

Twisting her torso round, Pat found she could dangle her weak legs over the side of the bed. She was dressed in a thin hospital gown. She placed both hands by her sides and tentatively rose up into a standing position. She stood for a few moments, adjusting as her head swam.

After some time, the tough little woman began taking small steps towards the door. Miraculously, it opened.

There was a long corridor punctuated with numbered doors, all dark save for one corridor light above her. Taking note of her room number 11, she began an uncertain walk towards the gloom. There was no natural light making it impossible to estimate the time. The electric lighting, sensitive to her presence, flickered on one by one as she descended the corridor.

Rooms 9, 7 and 5 passed on her left and the even rooms to her right. She stopped outside number 2. What was behind these doors? Was this a new section of the hospital she'd not visited before? It seemed strange as Pat was very familiar with the hospital wing; she had taken a number of patients there from the praise group and had worked numerous nursing shifts.

Turning to room 2, Pat twisted the doorknob but was disappointed to find it locked. She strained to hear. Was there movement behind it? Moving opposite, she attempted room 3, subconsciously hoping for either someone she knew or an abandoned packet of cigarettes.

It was locked.

All of a sudden, footfalls. Pat froze, suddenly guilty. Stepping away from the door, she made an instant decision. The corridor light above would have already given her away; therefore it made sense to continue walking purposefully down the corridor. She needed a cigarette and possibly a coffee, neither of which were forthcoming in her current situation.

At room 1, the corridor appeared to stop, however as Pat approached and the next corridor light flickered on, she realised that it actually turned a sharp 90 degrees to the right. Following the corridor round she saw light in the near distance and two figures approached dressed in white overalls.

"Madam?" said one.

Pat continued to walk towards them. As she did so she noticed one door to her right was ajar, enough that she could see quite clearly a lady was standing

right up close, looking out. They locked eyes for a moment then the door shut with a soft click.

"Madam? State your number." Pat stopped, confused.

"My number? My room number? It's room 11."

The two figures were strangely familiar, both female, both incredibly similar to each other, middle aged, hard faced. Hair swept back fiercely.

Pat squinted in disbelief and gave herself a firm pinch on her left forearm. It hurt. She was not dreaming. The two women walking down the corridor towards her were in fact, both Mother Pascal. Pat had never seen Pascal in anything other than the traditional nuns' habit but even with the strange white overalls and exposed hair, both women were still unmistakable. She must have had a twin all this time, working away here in this strange part of the Abbey that even Pat had no clue about.

"Patricia? You will need to return to your room now. You will receive refreshments and further instructions from there. It is 4am; you are up far too early. Go back."

The 'Go back' was almost barked.

Pat's brow furrowed. She was used to Mother Pascal's schoolmistress manner, of course she was, but this was altogether more peculiar..

"I never knew you 'ad a sister Mother Pascal?"

"Go back!"

The two women repeated the command in unison.

"Go back!"

"Alright, alright. Can you not talk to me a bit first? Alright it's a bit early, but yer up now, so we may as well chew the fat a bit till breakfast. What's yer sister's name? Is this a new wing of the 'ospital? I'm amazed I never saw it before, surely this place ain't got no secrets from ol' Pat?"

The two sisters, with expert precision managed to grab Pat's two upper arms and sail along the corridor with her in the middle like a convict on the way to trial.

224

"Hey now, this won't do!" Pat protested,

"I ain't done nothin!"

"You are to stay in your room and await further instruction. You have been unwell. You need rest."

"I'm right as rain, you can see I'm alright... I can walk you know, no need to get rough. I need a coffee though, coffee an' a fag."

Pat was pushed roughly enough that she stumbled into room 11. Whisking round to the door, she heard it shut and a key turned.

"I need a coffee!" she shouted through the keyhole,

"an' a cig!"

Silence, save an electrical humming and her own breathing. Well, hey, this was different. It was the first time she had felt a prisoner at the Abbey, from a sanctuary to jail. However, she supposed it could only be temporary. She had obviously been unwell, had gone through some sort of treatment and was now in recovery. It was expected that she would be separated from her work team as she healed... wasn't it?

She moved to her bed and sat, reaching for the water jug, she filled the beaker and took a swig. Lukewarm but ok. Replacing the beaker she noticed slight bruising around her inner wrist, looking closely she saw a small wound. She must have had an IV during her blackout. What time had passed? Surely ,a person returning to consciousness would have a slow and wobbly return to health. She had walked, albeit slowly, but she'd walked down that corridor. Maybe that was why no one had bothered to lock her door in the first place as they knew she could not possibly have risen up out of her bed. Feeling slightly shivery, Pat climbed under the covers. 7am was a good few hours away and if she could get a little rest before then, so much the better.

Charlotte stood aligned to the trunk of a large horse chestnut tree. She had seen a small group of figures in the distance walking from the underground Research centre towards the Abbey. With care, she could shelter completely from being seen and at the same time relive a bit of her childhood by reaching down to pick up the beautifully scented yet fiercely spiked conkers. One by one, she gently released the polished mahogany seeds, some huge singles filling the white leathery space and many twins with flat sheer edges that Charlotte ran her thumbs across again and again. She felt a certain peacefulness wash over her, the power of these transient things that would dull and roughen over the passing days. No one but her was a party to their birthing.

The first shock of white against the richest brown, something that had delighted generations of kids before and after her, adults too. Taking a small handful in her pocket she left the tree and crept carefully along to the hedgerow until she could get close enough to the hollybush.

For the first time, Charlotte felt glad about the dark regulation clothing, her former red cotton shirt would have shone out like Rudolf's shiny nose. She needed to know the time. The service was to last two hours but it was impossible to know how long she had been on the run. The Abbey clock was prominent, though not visible from her location. A cluster of distant voices carried on the wind as it changed direction and Charlotte quickly dived behind a spiky, unpleasant-looking bush peppered with abandoned spider nests. Squinting into the rain, she saw the small group walking with large umbrellas. They gathered by the main Abbey entrance. The Prime minister and one of the Arabian men walked in first followed by the remaining party. Charlotte supposed that the kind security officer took one last scan of the outside, his eyes resting a moment on her spiky bush before turning his back and entering the Abbey.

Some time passed.

Soaked through and starting to shiver again, Charlotte eased her way to the meeting place. Tucking herself into the base of the holly bush meant that she had minimal shelter from the wind and rain. Smoothing down her hair, she pulled the headscarf back up onto her head. She was going to look very wet, but with a bit of luck, the congregation would get soaked too as they left the Abbey.

With a sudden bang, the double doors flew open. Two security officers stood at either side as the people began to file out in pairs and threes. Charlotte found it hard to determine who was who, the recent regulation clothing made everyone look nearly identical and without height to guide her, she supposed she would never have spotted Jasmine. The sports coaches, teachers, lecturers, and gardeners all came out together, the scientists, the librarians, finally the carers... there they were, the lowest in the hierarchy, some of the Praise group were amongst them, the ones who could be trusted to remain silent. There she was, Jasmine a good head above the others. Charlotte felt palpable relief. She was safe.

"I got you a gift!"

"Oh yeah?" Jasmine smiled as the two reunited friends walked together.

Reaching into her concealed pocket, she pulled out three conkers and cupped them in her hands.

"These beauties are yours!"

"What, am I seven?!" she giggled with relief.

"I thought you'd come with a key to a secret crypt beneath our cabin, or a pair of diamond earrings... or the Prime Minister's underpants... or... or..."

"What do you take me for?!" Charlotte noticed Jasmine's eyes flicking to the wound on her face as her giggles faded.

"What are you going to do about that? About him?'

"I don't know. He took me by absolute surprise."

Jasmine nodded, concern etched across her face

"I've always thought he was a sullen and dark sort of... well... wanker really, but it seems he has a newfound confidence. I'll have to keep my wits about me."

"I noticed in the service he seemed to be scanning the crowds looking for someone. I hope he wasn't looking for you. Having said that. It'd be pretty easy to disappear dressed in this lot, so I'm absolutely certain that your cover wasn't blown..."

The two young women headed towards the kitchens, ready to help Mr Romano prepare the evening meal.

"He wouldn't have known," muttered Charlotte.

"Anyway, aside from conker collecting and rambling about the countryside like an absolute child, what else did you get up to? Anything constructive?!"

Charlotte smiled. "Well actually, yes. I may have unearthed some rather fascinating information about our Abbey, information that has remained secret for, I suspect, a very long time."

"Yes?"

"It's a bit mind blowing actually, incredibly surreal and..."

"Can you get to the bloody point?!" Jasmine snapped.

"If you haven't noticed, we start work in five minutes."

"It's momentous. I don't know if I can actually cover it in five minutes…"

"Try!"

Jasmine took her friend by the arm.

"Try!" she repeated earnestly.

Mr Romano bustled noisily about grabbing pans, changing his mind and slamming them back into the cupboards.

"You wanna something done…" he muttered.

Charlotte and Jasmine slipped over the threshold.

"Afternoon, Mr Romano!"

He stopped, a pan in each hand.

"Aha! My lovely staff! Good afternoon! Good afternoon indeed!"

He smiled, then stopped. His face transformed in a moment.

"What is zis? You are hurt, Carlotta?"

"I'm ok, Mr Romano, I'm ok." She smiled at him, grateful for his concern.

"You are not ok Carlotta. You need some ice or compress, something to take down the swelling. Jasmine? Freezer 4 top shelf, grab the peas. We 'ave much to do this afternoon, we need all the team in fighting form."

Minutes later, the two friends were flying about the kitchen rinsing onions in the oversized colander, grating carrots, slicing potatoes, preparing salads, stirring coleslaw. All the while, snippets of whispered conversation passed between them. Jasmine's face betraying her shock amid the steam from the pans. A strong scent of garlic cut through the air with a hiss.

"Jasmine, Carlotta, come 'ere one moment." Romano wiped his hands down his already filthy apron, then lifted it to mop his brow.

"Jack, saute these, and watch the stock! I come back in two minutes."

Jack arrived and took over. Romano gestured for the two women to go to the stockroom out the back, where the cool air hit them reassuringly. Romano continued to wipe his brow and cleared his throat a few times. They gathered in the semi-darkness by the sacks of onions and potatoes.

"Girls, I can see there are a changes 'appening all over the place and I don't know how you are finding this, but I want you two to understand that Romano is here for you if you need. I don't know if you are being knocked about or what is going on, but if you need a safe place, you come here. Always you can come here. Comprende?"

Charlotte felt a surge of compassion for this overstressed, overworked chef who, in the midst of dinner preparations, had come away just to emphasise that he had their back.

"Mr Romano, I can't thank you enough, really appreciate it," Charlotte stammered gratefully.

"Thank you Mr Romano," nodded Jasmine Mr Romano's eyes flicked briefly to the door

"Zis one Jasmine! Not zis one!" He snapped suddenly.

"Spanish onions are much bigger, you are 'alf asleep! You both!" He growled in feigned disgust, stomping back towards the door where they had come from.

Charlotte took the cue and instantly stooped to pick up a large bag of onions

"Are you going to help me or what?!"

The women took an end each of the huge bag before they became aware of Mr Romano in a heated exchange with another man. They walked precariously towards him till he and Mr Wilks burst into view.

"No! No! No! These girls! I say get the onion they get the 'ole bag! Per l'amor di Dio!" He performed an exaggerated gesture of frustration before turning to Wilks and saying,

"No sadly not Mr Wilks, I need these two in the kitchen," gesticulating to Jasmine three fingers.

"Three onions! Not three bags!"

He patted Mr Wilks with exaggerated affection about the shoulders.

"Come back later, my ol' friend, once these kids are away and the washing up done. It is time then for a nice drink."

Mr Wilks visibly stiffened at Mr Romano's over-intimacy.

Chapter 23

A black coffee, toast and a packet of cigarettes were placed beside the replenished water jug.

"It is the morning now Patricia. You need to try some breakfast."

Pat opened her eyes cautiously. She was resurfacing from a very peculiar dream that still left her anxious. The act of waking threatened to conceal some great secret that currently lay dormant within the dream, only just out of reach.

"You have toast to try. Should you require more, ring the bell."

Pat groaned with frustration as the secret vaporised. Rubbing her eyes, she saw a white figure moving in the direction of the door.

"Hey wait!"

The door shut with a soft click.

"Christ's sake," Pat muttered.

The still warm toast was divine, the coffee extraordinary, the cigarettes... a plain black box. Pat tapped one out and used the small lighter to bring it to life.

She took a deep drag, filling her lungs with the curling grey smoke. She held it there, the tobacco working its magic. The delayed exhalation brought with it a giddy catharsis. Well! These were exquisite! Never, Pat mused, had a fag tasted so good. With each puff, she felt as if she was lifting up outside of her body and into a tranquil state of mindfulness. By the fourth puff, Pat was euphoric, the toast crumbs and empty coffee cup looked like sculptural works of art.

Two scientists smiled appreciatively at the domestic scene unfolding on the screen.

"She's on cloud nine, that one," smiled the moustached man.

"She still appears rational though, no apparent loss of cognitive ability. Time perception may have waned a bit. Look she's just staring at the coffee cup. Will she snap out of it, do you think?"

"Why would she want to?" chortled the man.

Pat took one last drag, extinguished the cigarette and flopped back on the bed. She closed her eyes and allowed herself to drift slowly down from the play park of cherubs, through the white clouds and back into the room.

"If it were down to me, you'd have kicked that filthy habit of yours long ago," snapped a familiar voice.

"Repulsive smelling things. You are fortunate Mr Stramford insisted that you were allowed to keep on smoking as you please."

Pat opened her eyes for the second time that morning and felt pleasantly alert. She sprang up out of the bed to find Mother Pascal placing folded sheets in a neat pile.

"Well, Mr Stramford was a smoker, weren't he? Kindest man I ever met."

Pat paused as she thought of his last few words to her as he lay dying in the hospital wing of the Abbey.

"I dunno about normal smokin' bein' a filthy habit, but I tell you what, them cigarettes are somethin' else. What's in 'em? They're amazi"

Mother Pascal frowned and studied Pat hard.

"I believe Mr Stramford may have had a team working on a healthier alternative to smoking, I'm not sure whether that is what you just tried, either way, it's of little interest to me. You will need to gather all the positive energy you can muster for the line of work you'll be entering into now."

"What?"

"You are no longer to stay in the cabin with the other carers, you have been promoted to the highest order of the care team. I suppose you must have impressed the late Mr

Stramford, or maybe it's fate, but your duties are to change from this day forward."

"What are ye talkin' about?" Pat furrowed her brow.

"I got ill, I've just woke up 'ere and now you're tellin me I've been promoted? I don't want promotions at my age love. I want an easy life an' a garden."

"It is not down to you to decide your future."

The two women looked directly into each other's eyes, there was some sort of mutual understanding exchanged. Pat lowered her voice.

"When ye said I need positive energy, what were ye talkin' about?"

Pascal looked away from Pat and brushed non-existent crumbs from her white overalls.

"Ow come you've been away n'all? I can't say we exactly missed you... and I never knew you 'ad a twin sister."

Pascal looked back sharply.

"You are to take on another patient, one altogether more complex than those you have been used to."

"Well, the Praise group were pretty bloody complex."

"Refrain from bad language. It will not be tolerated. You have a new patient who is... who is dear to me."

Pascal quietened and her face looked momentarily afflicted, much to Pat's surprise.

"Dear to you? I don't mean to be rude, but I didn't think you was... capable." She stopped and instantly regretted her words.

"I'm sorry, I didn't mean that, I'm sure you 'ave people dear to yu like everyone else, other than our almighty God of course."

"The patient you are to support is in a state of high anxiety. She needs reassurance and compassion, but it is your direct, straight talking approach which is most likely to benefit her in the long term. As she progresses, she will be allowed greater freedoms, eventually joining the other residents in the Abbey."

"Is she a special guest? By that, what I mean... is she connected?"

"Yes."

"Not bein' funny but the Abbey has been housin' powerful people for years now. Why's this one any different?"

"Because she knows."

"Knows what?"

"She has worked out for herself... what I am about to tell you."

Pat gazed in astonishment at the size of the complex as they walked together through a large canteen, several corridors with spacious bespoke fitted bedrooms. There was no natural lighting at all, but the air felt fresh and clean and what lighting was visible was pleasantly tasteful. She had asked numerous questions, but Pascal had answered none.

Finally, seated in rather luxurious fabric chairs, Pascal crossed her legs and turned slightly in her seat so she was directly opposite Pat.

"I think it best that I begin. You need to process what you can without resorting to firing questions at me unless invited to do so. Is that clear?"

"Not to be provocative or anythin' but ain't conversations just s'posed to flow naturally. I mean, I like askin' questions, it usually tells me what I need to know. If I ain't allowed to ask 'em when I want, I'll probably have forgotten what the question even was."

"Thank you."

Pascal raised a severe eyebrow,

"I am now ready to begin." Pat resisted grimacing and instead sat patiently waiting.

"As you know, Stramford Abbey is at the forefront of medical research. You will have realised this over the years of working with the Praise group over at the Abbey buildings.

Pain relief particularly has been used to reduce the suffering of all our residents no matter the severity of their conditions.

"What you will not have realised is that the Abbey has also conducted significant blue-sky research projects in many advanced fields the finer details of which are not relevant to you, however, they need to be undertaken in the research centre and slowly integrated into the Abbey buildings, your former residence."

"Former? I definitely ain't going back then?"

"Not in the near future."

"Oh."

"So, occasionally the research results in 'situations' which can be troublesome for the scientists and need delegated to the white coats so that the research can continue unhindered."

"I dunno what you're on about." Pascal exhaled sharply in frustration.

"Ok, let's just cut to the chase here. A significant part of the research here involves stem cell technology. Do you know what that is?"

"Yes, that's where you can take stem cells from an embryo and grow a baby, ain't that right? I'm sure it was on the news a while back. Couldn't they grow any part of a human from these cells? An ear, an arm, even organs and things, imagine growing a set of lungs. I reckon I could probably do with a fresh new pair. It was bloody fascinatin' if I remember rightly. A bit Frankenstein-y, a bit futuristic, but pretty amazin' nonetheless."

Pascal forced a stiff smile.

"Thank you. So, you have certainly heard of some of the headlines surrounding its possibilities. Since the Abbey's early research into neurological injuries and neurodegenerative disorders, whereby the scientists were able to explore effective treatments for the likes of Parkinsons and so on, further experiments enabled the effective growth of new organs, numerous trials took place over the years and lately the results were so successful that the scientists have been able to complete an exact clone of a living person."

Pat scrunched up her eyes for a moment as she studied Pascal.

"How's that sit with your Christian faith? I ain't sure that cloning humans is even legal, is it? It's like the most unethical thing you can do, right?"

"You will remember that I outlined the format for questions at the start of this interview."

"Interview?!"

"So, I will continue. You saw my sister back in the corridor yesterday. She is not in fact, my sister. She is my clone. We are genetically identical."

"Are you actually 'avin' a laugh?" Pascal glowered at Pat.

"Alright, you ain't 'avin' a laugh. Alright... Let me just think about this... How do I know you're the real Mother Pascal? How long has this clonin' thing been going on? Are there any other clones wanderin' about? Are there any grizzly side effects? Oh lord, this is just mad!"

"You will remember Tilly? Our burns victim."

"Course I know Tilly."

"Her parents are currently in talks with the Abbey with regard to Tilly's release back to her home pending treatment for her injuries."

Pat looked at Pascal.

"The Abbey ain't going to grow a new hand and a fresh new skin for her are they?"

"No... well it's just plausible that they could, but they won't." "I'm guessin' that's what they've promised though, right?"

"The Stephensons will have their daughter back exactly as she looked before. She was a beautiful young woman with plenty more life to live."

"So I'm guessin' they'll just use our Tilly's stem cells to grow another Tilly that ain't burnt to shit."

"Language!" Pascal flared angrily.

"And I'm guessin' the Stephenson's won't hold back with their purses?! Ain't they multi-millionaires or something? I'm sure Tilly told me her dad was involved in oil or somethin'."

"Each family's circumstances are not our concern."

"So, can I ask questions yet?"

"No. I am not finished."

"You're gonna tell me I'm lookin' after the burnt, forgotten about Tilly, the one the parents don't want."

"No! You are not listening. The parents will have their only daughter returned to them. They are not rejecting anyone."

"Oh, come on! Listen to yourself!" Pat paused suddenly. "They're not going to euthanise our Tilly, are they?"

"No. They need her alive and well, should her parents have any future requirements further down the line."

"Jesus Christ... this is like a God-awful 1950s Sci-Fi film."

"Will you stop using our Lord's name in vain?!" Pascal snapped fiercely.

"It is our Lord and Father that you will need to seek in these difficult times

ahead. He works in mysterious ways and it is not our place to question Him. It is downright sinful to use His name in vain, especially as you will need His guidance more than ever."

"You're right, I shouldn't. You're right... Mr Stramford did show me God's way all them years ago and it's made me who I am today," Pat murmured.

"Do not forget it then!"

There followed a long silence where both women looked away from each other, apparently lost in thought. Pat finally broke the silence.

"I can 'ave another smoke, can I?... maybe outside? It's a lot of information to take in, right? I don't think you've told me the half of it neither."

"Not outside. You stay here within the walls of the Research Centre now... and indefinitely."

"Not outside?! You mean never?!" Pat was suddenly furious.

"All my 'ard work out in the grounds tendin' the gardens, training up all them red shirts designing and physically managin' the groundworks, are you actually kiddin' me?!"

"You surprise me Patricia. You've already been given the luxury of cigarettes, yet apparently it is not good enough. You have become selfish as a result of all your freedoms. Please remember others before yourself."

Pat wanted to ball her fist and thump it smack across Pascal's cheek. What an intolerable woman, so self-righteous and condescending. Instead, she forced herself to stay calm and uncurled her fist to reach for the cigarettes in her thin hospital gown pocket. She struck a match and lit one. Taking a long drag, she looked intensively at Mother pascal. "You said you 'ad more to tell me, so go on."

Pascal's lip curled with dislike for either Pat or the cigarette smoke as it unfurled about them.

"You are not working with Tilly as talks remain ongoing and Tilly will not be made aware of her situation until all the legalities are finalised. I believe the parents have to sign a gagging order of some sort to exonerate The Abbey's involvement in her treatment other than spiritual healing of course. If the parents do choose to pay whatever fee has been proposed, then yes Tilly will require much care as she will be taken over to the research centre indefinitely and will no longer have any contact with her family at all."

"Because they won't know she's even here. The Tilly clone that accompanies them home is their daughter, as far as they're aware... That's pretty sick, isn't it? I don't think that sits well with our faith, right Pascal?"

"Right, let us straighten something out here very clearly,"

Pascal almost growled.

"I am not here to defend the workings of this institution. As you well know, I am (To use Stramford's founding words) a cog in a well-oiled machine, just as you are. Equally, I cannot discuss ethical or religious concerns with you or anyone else. These are personal concerns that can be dealt with through private prayer. You have been shown how to talk to our Lord God, so it is your responsibility to use that to both inspire and heal you. Do not ask any further questions about my opinions or faith on this matter. Is that understood?"

Pat took a long drag on her cigarette and nodded.

"Tilly is a good example to use so you can understand the complexities of this side of the Abbey. The part you came from was all about spiritual healing, and showing our residents the light via sport, music and art. Those rich facilities are there because of the money generated over here on this side. The Research centre is generating big business from wealthy people, desperate for themselves and their loved ones to be healed or fixed... A tennis court isn't going to cure Parkinsons, the stables may bring so much joy to our residents, but they can't cure cancer. All this has been going on for decades. Some rich and powerful punters were happy to pay solely for their loved ones to pass away peacefully and without pain, others fought to cure them... but this new stem cell technology has enhanced the Abbey's possibilities tenfold."

Pascal paused to gather herself.

"The reason you are here, in the Research Centre is because you have been raised under Mr Stramford's ethos, you show compassion for the residents and The Abbey runs through your veins."

Pat let out a sigh.

"Probably would've been better to keep me head down then."

"No, no, just before Stramford died, a plan was set out, one in which a highly efficient new team was to be set up in the Research Centre. Prior to this, it has only been scientists and mathematicians, engineers and so on, but now with this new technology, there is a need for people management. There will potentially be an influx of 'Tilly's that will need to be cared for to enable long term investment from the wealthiest partners."

Pat gave a sort of shrug and said quite weakly. "Look m'love. I dunno that I need to know all that, There ain't nothin' I can do with all that information other than to get stressed with it. In a nutshell, what your tellin' me is I've left my old Abbey quarters and I'm now over 'ere carin' for some poor sods while the Abbey clone them off and give 'em back to their parents... spouses... whatever."

"Yes, very simply... you've understood. Just two things remain outstanding."

"Alright, hit me with it."

"Firstly... your patient is Mrs Pauline Nkosi, the wife of our current Prime Minister."

"My God, really?!" stammered Pat.

Mother Pascal raised her eyes up to the heavens and her jaw twitched as if she was suppressing some inner turmoil. Taking a deep breath as if to recover, she spoke again, calm and collected.

"In order to enable you to complete all your duties effectively... you too, have been cloned."

Chapter 24

Two women in white lab coats swept down the corridor. Using eye recognition technology, the large secure door swung open and they walked through. They were met by a moustached man also in white. The small group moved through a large lounge area in deep discussion.

"She was surprisingly compliant, I faced very little resistance at all." "To be expected."

The three entered the science laboratory. A large machine emitted loud hissing sounds and shuddered before falling silent. Several scientists moved swiftly amongst huge freezer units. One man perspiring heavily, shouted across the lab. From a sealed metal pod in the middle of the room, two figures burst out of the heavy door carrying a large plastic tank between them. There was a clear plasma-like liquid surrounding something fleshy. The sweating man ran up towards the small goats' enclosure and shouted.

"They're in the pod! Is it fucking open day today!? Bring over a white coat! Yes YOU, you fucking numskull!!"

The goats scattered in fright, clanging the bars of their small pen, then regrouped, bleating weakly.

The three white figures passed across the laboratory to reach another secure door on the opposite side. This one closed with a vacuum seal. The intensive noise of the working environment was replaced with a airport lounge calm, a thick patterned carpet and framed works of art between doors fixed with brass numbers. Some had name plates. A full-size grand piano took up the faraway corner. There were no windows. Dominating the room was a large oak table with twelve heavy chairs surrounding it. Seated were Bim Nkosi and the Sheikh. The third person bore a striking resemblance to the two approaching ladies in white coats, though she wore a traditional nuns' habit. The moustached man extended his hand to the Prime Minister and greeted the Sheikh with a warm embrace.

"Gentlemen," the corners of his moustache lifted.

Bim Nkosi had removed his tie completely and loosened his collar. His jacket hung propped on the back of his chair and sweat marks were prominent under his arms and down his back.

"I understand this has been an exceptionally strange day for you sir," said the man, with concern.

"You could say that..." sighed the Prime Minister, twisting his wedding band distractedly around his finger.

"I see here you have requested a full report as to the..."

"Good grief! More Heathers!" Interrupted Bim with a shallow laugh which hung uncomfortably in the air.

The two white coated Pascals nodded respectfully while the seated Mother Pascal cleared her throat to speak.

"Bim, we are all essentially the same person, you can trust us as one. We all know you and Pauline equally, as our memories are intertwined."

Bim grimaced.

"How exactly does that work?"

"We are exact genetic copies of each other. All memories and past living experiences are shared. We were created at the same time, four of us in total."

"Four?!"

"Yes Mr Nkosi, four at present. Each one of us knows the work of the Abbey inherently therefore, our duties are logical and do not need to be learned. New information is delivered to us in a way that allows us to process and utilise the data effectively. We hold the same strong Christian faith that both you and Pauline are familiar with. Nothing has changed about my character, it is just that there are now more of me and our increased ability to ensure the smooth running of this institution."

"So how long have... have you all been in existence?"

Pascal made to answer, but the Prime Minister interrupted by raising his hand.

"No don't tell me... it was just before Michael died, wasn't it? That's why you couldn't come to see Pauline... when she was so upset..."

Bim looked distracted for a moment. "Can I see Pauline now? Is she okay?"

Both white coated women made to speak, but one stopped so that the other could continue.

"We have just left Pauline sleeping in her room. She is recovering well from the physical effects of such an acute emotional trauma, however she is tired and we request that she stays just a few days more so that we can monitor her progress. All being well, she will return to full health and will be able to accompany you back to London."

Pascal glanced across at the Sheikh and back to the Prime Minister.

"I understand there are some legal requirements to be signed before her release. I'm not sure of the exact details. A non-disclosure agreement?"

"Thank you, Madam. We are seeing to that just now." The Sheikh frowned and made a gesture as if to dismiss the two ladies.

"Before you are going, fetch this man a drink. What would you like, sir? A lighter beer, perhaps? What would refresh you before we are to undertaking the legal papers, this and that."

He waved his hand as if conducting.

Bim sighed and massaged his temples.

"I feel like Alice in Wonderland here. I half expect you to tell me those goats in the laboratory can speak the King's English... but supposing they can't and I am in fact just very tired I'll take a brandy if you have such a thing, I would also like a pint glass full of cold lemonade just to hydrate myself again. If you would be so kind Heather?"

The two white coated Heather Pascals left through a numbered door.

Pat was taken back to her room but felt horribly contained and couldn't suppress her nervous energy.

"What am I s'posed to do now? Where is everythin'? 'Ow come there ain't no windows? Where's the canteen? Where's anyone else?"

She had tried these questions and others on the stern Mother Pascal but nothing gave. The hard-faced woman stayed resolute and silent. Finally as they went through the last doorway to the corridor that Pat had tentatively explored that very morning. Pascal stepped back and allowed the door to shut between them.

"Hey! HEY!"

Pat growled to herself.

"All the people in the Abbey an' I end up stuck with multiple copies of that old cow with a metal rod up 'er arse."

She looked bleakly at the numbered doors. She had absolutely no intention of entering her new bedroom again, she was fractious and full of energy, a feeling she recognised that often occurred just as she began her gardening duties. Oh, her garden! Misery pulled at her heart.

"God's sake," she scowled and stood with her back to the tightly locked door.

"You're a coward, you're a cowardly fraud- that's what ye are Pascal!" she roared, bringing on a shuddering cough.

"A bloody coward, yeah you are."

She reached into the pocket of her hospital gown and withdrew the cigarette packet.

"At least somebody loved me," she muttered.

A sharp click came from one of the doors, four doors down from where she stood. A rather unkempt mop of grey hair atop a crinkled face appeared around the door.

Pat took a step forward.

"Who's that?"

The figure stepped out and the face broke into a delighted smile.

"No way!"

"God, ain't you gorgeous?!"

The two identical grey-haired women walked slowly up to each other, their eyes devouring each other's every detail.

"You're my flippin' clone! My God, Look at yu!" A big grin matching her twin's stretched across her face.

"I dunno what to think!"

"Jesus, ain't this weird?! Let me see the back of me 'ead, turn around, come on! I thought I was better lookin' than that!"

The two women laughed then stopped suddenly, both equally shocked by the sound of the other's identical voice.

"So...what's your name then?"

"It's Pat, you fuckin' idiot!"

The two burst into laughter again.

"Alright Patty, I'll stay as Pat if it's all the same to you."

"No it ain't! You know fine Ma called me Patty and I don't want that never."

Both ladies became sober, both reliving the exact same memory but able to etch that wound on the face of the other. They stopped close to each other and tapped each other's shoulders both fondly and nervously at the same time.

"I'll 'ave a ciggy too, if you've got one spare?" Said the cigarette-less one.

255

"Course, course!" said Pat, hastily pulling out her cigarette packet but all the time not allowing her eyes to leave her new sister.

"You know what a shit show we're in now, right?" said one.

"Yeah, yeah it ain't good. Seems like we 'ave to live like rats under the groun' or bats in a cave."

"No more sun, no more gardenin'. All them little birds that used to hop over and eat the worms that I dug up. The breeze that rustled all the autumn leaves abou'. We won't see them mini pink and white cyclamen that popped up in the grass. No more squeaky wheelbarrow, no more friends... it's a proper shit show."

Both women stopped talking and wandered small circles, gazing into nothingness.

"It's the first sign of madness ye know."

"Talkin' to yersel, yeah I know."

Pat extinguished her cigarette on the bottom of her shoe and popped the butt into the cigarette box. She looked across at her clone, whose eyes twinkled back at her.

Chapter 25

Charlotte turned on the tap and watched the water swirl round the basin and gurgle down the plug hole. Cupping her hands together as if accepting communion, she filled them and splashed the chilly water over her face. It woke her. She felt stray drips travelling down her neck and into her collar.

With the hand towel about her neck, she wandered back into the cabin and felt her eyes drop to the bed that used to belong to Pat.

Bernadine and Jasmine had moved to the other two beds and though the room was very much inhabited, it still held an emptiness for Charlotte. The window that opened and shut numerous times a day so Pat could smoke remained mostly shut. All Charlotte's fiery tantrums that had been expertly closed down by a look or a smart word already fading into memories. That broad-shouldered but small grey-haired lady with her twinkly eyes and terrible smoking habit had brought a lot of humour and good old fashioned banter to Charlotte's often cynical outlook. That and something else. Something altogether more dignified.

"What time are we supposed to leave the Praise group today?" Jasmine asked no one in particular. There was a short silence, where Charlotte showed no sign of having heard her friend.

"My morning notifications say half an hour earlier than usual. There's staff coming to cover us, so I'd imagine when they appear, we disappear."

Bernadine said, brushing her long hair and pulling it into a low tail.

"What do you think they're up to? Switching us all around again? I hope we're given more time at the stables. I know Romano is awesome, but I hate the sweaty heat of the kitchen and would much rather shovel horse shit than scrape dinner plates."

Jasmine yawned without inhibition.

"Oh I dunno, at least the time goes quick."

Charlotte suddenly replied.

"I kind of like the busyness of the kitchen and there's always people coming and going... it's kinda sociable... kinda safe."

"That's just cos you're a social butterfly! Yapping to everyone that'll listen, confiding in old Romano and getting all the Abbey gossip! Nah, give me the peace of a stable yard any day. Just me, the horses, and a brush. Sounds like paradise."

"Yeah perhaps... if you're not looking over your shoulder for a sex crazed, power hungry..."

"Wanker," intervened Bernadine quietly.

Both Jasmine and Charlotte spun round in amazement.

"She didn't?"

"She did!"

The two young women crouched beside their friend as she sat on the bed. A pregnant pause lingered.

"D'you want to tell us what's been going on?"

"No," Bernadine said resolutely,

"Though I now feel quite at liberty to call a spade a spade... and a wanker, a wanker."

Charlotte's lips twitched with amusement.

"What on earth has brought this on Bernadine? I mean, I'm delighted, I'm so happy you can talk... I mean, we're here for you. Always... I mean I don't think we've got oodles of time to discuss stuff now, but we will... we absolutely..."

"Charlotte, shut up." Jasmine snapped.

"Bernadine? You were saying..."

"Thank you. Thank you both. I know you have always tried to protect me. I may talk a little bit later. I may not. Either way, we really have to get to Praise group. Oh, but you both absolutely must know. There is a means to protect yourself from harm, which I discovered quite by accident." Bernadine lifted her small face up to look at them both as her cheeks flushed with pride.

"It was through talking to Pat just before she disappeared... she showed me how to make my tablet computer sound an alarm."

"An alarm?"

"Yes. Patricia showed me with reference to Praise group, however I cannot be entirely sure but I suspect she was showing me for other reasons."

"Knowing Pat, that is very likely."

"So what is it then, this alarm?"

Bernadine took her tablet out of her pocket and showed both friends where a single semi-depressed button sat between the volume controls and power button.

"If this thin button here is pressed fully for three seconds, it will sound a very loud panic alarm. It's not possible to accidentally press it as it's hidden well on the device and I'm not that sure that anyone really knows about it because when... let's just say the opportunity arose to test it out... Mr Wilks face betrayed the fear of God. Never have I seen such terror in a face as his and he turned on his heel and ran from me like I had summoned the devil himself."

"Go Bernadine! You absolute legend! That's awesome!"

Charlotte smiled.

"But why do you think he had such a strong reaction? Do you think he

took that alarm to mean something else?" Jasmine frowned

"Well, whatever it meant to him, it worked very well. Now we've got to go. I've made us late!" The three women left the cabin.

A heart monitor beeped, something else beeped too, periodically speeding up and then slowing. The hum of something to the left appeared to inflate and then deflate something to the right. There were feet moving about. Sometimes they shuffled from the bottom of the bed right up to the top and Pauline Nkosi felt her wrist gently turn to face upwards, then the feet moved back to the foot of the bed again. This is a weird dream, she thought. The newly turned wrist throbbed uncomfortably before everything went black and sleep resumed.

The beeping resurfaced. Mechanical, rhythmical, comforting. Pauline allowed her eyelids to part just enough that she could see contorted shapes swim about through her eyelashes. It was tiring. She let her eyelids shut again.

She chose to listen instead, looking felt too hard. Blocking out the heart monitor and the inflating and deflating thing beside her, she tried to focus on other sounds.

The bottom of the bed, the sounds changed down there. They were irregular and interesting. Squeaks and creaks... was that a chair? The rustle of some sort of synthetic fabric. Was that a whisper? Pauline's ears pricked up. What did it say?

"How long are we talking here?" A deep voice suddenly pierced the soundscape. A quieter female voice answered from the far end of the room.

Pauline began to feel an uneasy alertness building behind her eyes. It hurt but she had to open them. She had to wake up. Again, fuzzy shapes appeared between her eyelashes. The male voice disappeared to the back of the room. Desperately, Pauline tried to focus on her fingers and her toes. Could she move them? No. She would have to burst out of this thick leaden blanket, suffocating her body and binding her limbs. Was she drugged? Panic rose like bile in her throat. Could she scream? Nothing.

Footsteps approached. A warm hand took her wrist and gently turned it so that it faced upwards. Blackness closed in once again.

Chapter 26

The Praise group wore aprons for a focused pottery session. Perched on stools they pulled up close to a table covered with large boards, wooden tools and great lumps of clay. There were varying degrees of success at bowls and pots. Jasmine was seated beside a small man who caressed his pot lovingly without taking his eyes away from it for a second. She felt tenderness. It was as if his clay treasure would spoil; dare he not give it his full undivided attention. Opposite him were two older ladies, both white haired, one heavier than the other. They appeared greatly amused by the whole experience and made numerous derogatory remarks about the other's pot until they'd feign fury, smash it in with a fist and begin the process again.

Charlotte stood at the sink, rinsing pots while Bernadine typed notes in the Praise group handover journal.

A light tap tap and Charlotte's father, Mr Compton, popped his head round the door.

"Charlotte, Jasmine." He nodded at them and stepped into the room.

"Tilly? Is Tilly here? Ok yes, and Bernadine, I need you too."

The small party followed Mr Compton down the corridor, out of the Praise group buildings and towards the sports complex. They entered the sliding doors and chlorine cut through the air sharply, giving Charlotte an unbidden nostalgia for childhood swimming lessons. They passed vending machines bulging with chocolate, protein snacks and crisps. Loud music pumped from a large gym with several people lifting weights. A prominent water cooler took up a corner as the group turned towards the badminton courts.

"You girls have two hours to yourselves to enjoy some badminton. Refreshments will be brought to you halfway through. There is all the equipment you need in the cupboard."

They slowed as Mr Compton pulled the heavy door.

"Here, in we go ladies."

He gestured for the women to follow him into the room. They saw a net and court markings, a beautifully high domed ceiling with a skylight at the highest point. It shone like a star with a dust cloud tail swirling in the disturbed air.

"As I said, you'll be quite busy here for a few hours and well done! You have obviously impressed someone to have earned such a treat as this when your counterparts are washing the dishes or some such!"

He smiled kindly, his eyes crinkling at the corners.

He moved to go,

"Oh! Before I forget. I'll need your devices so I can put them in the secure sports locker."

He extended his hand to the women who obediently handed over their devices. All but Tilly, who as a resident, had none.

Mr Compton propped his glasses on his head and while holding the 3 devices struggled with a set of keys. Finally, he took his own device and placed it on the top of the small locker box. With his free hand, he fumbled with the keys, eventually releasing the right one. Opening the small locker, he placed the three devices inside and locked it. Giving an affirmative nod, he moved to the door. It closed with a thud followed by the unmistakable sound of a bolt being slid across.

The four women looked at each other uneasily.

"A bit strange this, isn't it?" said Jasmine.

"It appears… It appears that we have been singled out and taken away… away from something, but what… and why?"

Charlotte's eyes rested briefly on top of the sports locker.

"You won't believe what my dad's gone and done. I swear he never learns…"

Reaching to the top of the locker, she pulled down her father's tablet. She swiped the screen and groaned.

"Thought it was too good to be true. He's put a PIN code on it."

Jasmine joined her friend.

"Well, come on now, genius. We've got some time to kill. How about you try a few pins out. It's only 4 digits right?"

"C'mon losers! Are you gonna play badminton or not? While you're faffing about wasting time on that thing, I'd love a game!"

With her one good hand, Tilly clutched the racket hard. She seemed to struggle with distance vision, having only one functioning eye, but it did not seem to curb her enthusiasm.

"Sure, I'll join you." Volunteered Bernadine.

A very gentle game ensued, Bernadine taking special care to ensure that the shuttlecock was always returned lightly and predictably back to Tilly's racketed hand. On the other hand, Tilly made an effort to strike the shuttlecock with a smash whenever possible.

"Come on! Stop babying me Bernadine! Give me something to do!!!"

Bernadine smiled kindly and made some attempts to hit the shuttlecock further away from her opponent, yet her face betrayed pity as she watched the wretched girl limp and hobble about the court.

"Oh whatever, I'm playing Charlotte, she doesn't care. Charlotte!" Tilly clutched her racket and started limping over.

"Yeah, wait. I'm trying to think," Charlotte said distractedly.

The four young women surrounded the device, Bernadine slightly back from the others.

"What are you looking for that's more damn important than playing a bit of badminton with me?!"

Tilly's face twisted up on one side attempting a cheeky smile, though it didn't and instead resulted in a 'Joker' grin, sinister and full of teeth.

"Shut up Tilly, I'll play in a sec," came Charlotte

"Your birthday, your dad's birthday, your mum's birthday, the date that she died... What else can it be?"

Charlotte looked blankly at Tilly. Beads of sweat had gathered at her brow, the thicker, yellower skin looked exaggeratedly different to her patches of unburned skin, which now blushed pink.

"I know... hang on. She tapped in four numbers."

The tablet unlocked and the home screen winked approvingly at them. "Yes! Oh YES! Get me!!!" Charlotte beamed at Jasmine, who looked astonished.

"Lemme guess... your dad's year of birth?" "No! You doughnut. My parents' wedding day."

Bernadine moved away and started to pick up stray shuttlecocks around the court. Within a moment, a sudden movement at the door. Before the young women had time to hide the tablet, the door swung open.

Mr Compton, Mr Wilks and two unknown figures stood in the doorway.

"My Tablet Charlotte," Mr Compton's face expressionless as he extended his hand.

Charlotte numbly handed the tablet over, all the elation of finding the pin draining away through her eyes, her neck and her chest until her stomach felt leaden. Guilty.

"Tilly, it is unfortunate that these women found it appropriate to use your extra recreation time as an excuse to infiltrate and pry upon senior management. This is not yours, Charlotte. Not everything you flippantly desire can become yours. Again, you have jeopardised the safety of those around you..."

Mr Compton appeared to be sweating excessively and took out a large white handkerchief to wipe his forehead.

"Because of your reckless, selfish desire to possess what is not yours."

Charlotte felt fury building about her abdomen. She tried to swallow it down and hard though it was, said nothing.

Mr Wilks scanned the four, pulling his eyes away prematurely from Tilly as if her burns burnt him. He scanned the other three slowly and cruelly, the faintest smirk upon his lips.

"Bernadine," he said at last.

"I'd have thought better of you."

Her eyes filled with tears and she looked down. Charlotte and Jasmine stood defiantly yet did not speak.

Finally, he beckoned Tilly to come to him, though she froze, unsure what to do.

"Come Tilly. There is no need for you to be punished because of their behaviour."

She stood her ground...

"You're alright. I'll stay here." She said, levelly.

Mr Wilks turned to the door and nodded at the two figures standing just out of sight. They walked over to Tilly. Taking a side each, they waltzed Tilly out of the room. Her good eye widened in surprise, yet she remained silent. Wilks followed the trio, banging the door shut behind him. The bolt slid across.

Charlotte turned immediately to Jasmine.

269

"Well... it could have been worse??"

Jasmine sighed and rolled her eyes.

"We didn't even find anything on the tablet... for all the fuss."

There was silence. Jasmine absent-mindedly picked up a badminton racket and gently tapped it against her knee.

"I wonder who that woman was? I also wonder what the hell punishment awaits us. God, I hate this place, it's like a goddamn boarding school."

She stopped tapping the racket for a moment.

"Why on earth did they take Tilly away?"

Charlotte shrugged, barely listening to her friend as if deep in thought. After some time, she picked up a racket and wandered into the centre of the court.

"I suppose we may as well have a game before the walls start closing in.... Or they release the rats. Or water starts rising up from our ankles to our necks!"

"Oh shut up! SHUT UP!!!" muttered Bernadine from across the court, furiously wiping tears from her eyes.

"Everything was so much better before you came along Charlotte. You've ruined everything! Everything!"

Had Charlotte a reproach, it was instantly lost as, just at that moment, a loud clunk extinguished the lights and blackness descended around them.

A whimper from Bernadine echoed spookily off the brick walls as Charlotte adjusted. She felt her eyes tugging about their sockets as they flailed uselessly about. Nothing to the left, to the right, behind, the front... just dense swirling black.

What about up? She tilted up her chin. Ah. There. A reassuring moon-like orb directly above.

Bernadine's whimpers turned to low wails.

"Look up Bernadine!" Charlotte called out into the darkness,

"Look up to the skylight."

The three women all looked up at the orb as if to ground themselves against the swirling black.

"Come here Bernadine!" Charlotte called towards where she last remembered seeing her.

"I can't... I can't see."

"Come towards my voice Bernadine! Jasmine, you're somewhere close to me right? You're nearby?"

"Yeah, I'm here. God this is dark."

An eerie cry came from Bernadine's direction.

"Fuck's sake, shut up! You're absolutely freaking me out Bernadine!"

A silence followed.

With attempted composure, Charlotte continued,

"The walls echo all over the place, I can't be doing with wailing. Your voice is bouncing back and forth. You just need to come here!"

Charlotte heard her echo bouncing about.

To the voyeur, the unfolding scene may have looked quite comical. Two ladies semi-crouching with their arms outstretched, waltzing around and around each other, just missing contact, until hand met thumb which became a clutching hold, two arms locked around the torso of the other and for a fraction, both took such comfort from the welcome warmth of another person that they embraced for some time.

"We have to get to Bernadine."

"Charlotte, I can't bloody see!"

"Pull yourself together. This is a badminton court. Some bugger is going to want to play badminton at some point and they'll turn the lights on."

"But I can't see! I can't see even the slightest anything. I'm completely blind."

"No Jas, they just turned the lights off, don't be so bloody dramatic."

It wasn't long before two became three. There was tangible relief as they all found each other.

Two long hours passed. They became cold and maudlin. Alternating between jogging on the spot and hugging each other to keep warm. Charlotte spoke of her discoveries during her escape from the memorial service.

"It was much colder outside in the monks' cells. This is paradise in comparison, with no gale and no blattering rain horizontally against your pathetically thin clothes. No risk of being seen!"

This provoked a small chuckle from Jasmine.

"I can't see my own feet, but I'm pretty certain that being seen is not our chief concern right now."

"I wish they hadn't turned the flipping heating off too. It's getting so cold."

Bernadine said nothing. Unbeknown to the others she was engaged in prayer, seeking comfort from God, her cold hands clasped together.

"I will need to tell you what I heard over in that monk's cell..." Continued Charlotte.

"I don't think even the staff over here know what's going on. It seems there's a whole different part of the Abbey under the ground. They're doing crazy scientific experiments, like cloning actual humans... cloning Jas. Is that mind numbing or what?"

"Cloning?" repeated Jasmine in disbelief.

"For what purpose? And why?" "Oh come on, why do people do anything? It's always for money, right?"

"But who? Who has been cloned? How the hell do they even do that?" Charlotte lowered her voice.

"You don't think I can be heard here, do you?" She whispered.

Chapter 27

"Mrs Nkosi. You need to wake now, m'love. It ain't doin' yu no favours lying down too long. It's Pat 'ere, it's Pat..."

Pauline smelt tobacco. It was nice. Familiar.

"You gotta get up, 'ave some food, get yu strength up a bit. You'll be fine, it's all gonna be fine."

With considerable effort, Pauline opened her eyes. There was a white polystyrene tiled ceiling. The setting was medical. With the bright visual clues returning, auditory ones flooded in, too. The repetitive beeping, the hum of equipment.

There was no window.

"Mrs Nkosi? There now. That's better. You're doin' remarkably well. Takes a little while to adjust, don't it? But you'll be right as rain in just a bit."

Pauline welcomed the clarity in her vision that had abandoned her during that dark time when she couldn't fight past her own eyelashes.

"Patricia? Is that you? You nursed Michael, you were kind to him. Where are you?"

"Try to turn your 'ead love, turn to find me voice."

With enormous effort, Mrs Nkosi finally managed to see Pat's kind face smiling at her.

"That weren't too bad, was it? You're over the worst, it's jus' strength to strength from 'ere."

With help from Pat and several cushions, Pauline was lifted to a seated position and ate tea and toast while surveying her surroundings.

"Where's Bim? Is he not coming to collect me soon?"

"Don't worry a jot about that, your focus is on gettin' better love."

Pauline turned suspiciously upon Pat and, taking upon a more authoritative tone, repeated the question.

"When is my husband coming to collect me?"

Pat started but stopped, half choked on a cough. Took a moment to recover and then said.

"I... er... I assume 'e'll be 'ere once you're better m'am."

"I think you can see that I am indeed better, therefore, I would like to speak with my husband now. Where is my handbag? My phone is in there. Where is my handbag?" The voice was laden with controlled anger.

"I will make enquiries to find yer 'andbag m'am but..."

"Enquiries?!" Pauline's eyes flashed dangerously.

"I mean, what I actually mean is I 'aven't a clue where your 'andbag is and... I won't make any sodding enquiries anyway."

The grey-haired lady shook her head sadly.

"I dunno what an enquiry even is, to be honest. All I can tell you... is that... is that you're in shit creek with the rest of us and if you act all haughty and stuff, you'll make this a whole lot bloody 'arder!"

A pronounced silence followed, and then, with an exasperated sigh, Pat stood up from the bedside chair and began clearing away the breakfast things.

Pauline took Pat's wrist as she cleared the empty butter paper and knife.

"You know... you know what I saw. You know my suspicions, don't you?"

"Aw... probably. I'm as tired of this shit as you are. I think you would do ten times better talking to Pascal, your ol' friend. I think you two see eye to eye or something, so she'd be way better explainin'..."

"Explaining what Patricia?"

"Explaining that scientific shit she already told me just a few days ago. It's too big to get me 'ead around and I don't care much either. I'm sorry, I'm so sorry for you. You seem nice... You didn't deserve this."

"Deserve what Patricia? What's going on? Is it that I saw a double of Heather Pascal? Is that it? I can keep that to myself if necessary. I can sign non-disclosure. It's no problem. Patricia? Pat? Why won't you look at me? Why... are you crying? Are you crying?"

"Oh, fuck's sake!" Pat drew a sleeve across her nose.

"This is too cruel. I jus' want yu to know. I ain't got no part of this other than I've found meself here just like you 'ave."

She let out a sob, then, as if embarrassed, turned it into a cough and reached into her pocket for a tissue.

"I shouldn't be doin' this on me own. I'm gonna screw up. Let me call someone..."

"No!" Pauline swung her legs round out of the bed.

She sat swaying slightly, hands gripping the side of the mattress.

"Please don't call anybody. I've been sedated long enough. I beg you, Patricia. Let me hear what you have to say and stay with me. Just you. Stay with me."

Pat took a few moments. She dried her eyes and blew her nose. She took the chair by the bedside again and sat with her elbows on her knees, head down as if in prayer.

"How abou' you ask me questions, then I can do me best to answer 'em. There's too much to make sense of and if I try and tell yu everythin' at once. It won't make no sense... And put yer feet back in the bed, love. You need t' keep warm. Yu need to recover."

"Is Heather Pascal dead?" "No."

"Has she got a double?" "Yeah."

"Am I able to see her?"

"Yeah. But she wanted you to see me first, so I could explain stuff to yu. I think she can't... or somethin'."

"Why can't she?"

"Coz you're friends and it... hurts 'er"

"But surely friends... I mean... So what do you have to explain to me?"

"Mother Pascal has been cloned."

There was silence as Pauline studied the funny little grey lady with intense green eyes as she said that simple statement.

"Cloned, you say? "Yeah."

"How? Here? In this medical centre?"

"Yeah."

"Okay, well, I suspected something like that. I assume it is entirely illegal and ethically incomprehensible. I suppose the delay in getting back to Bim is because I'll need to sign something to... But why... why did you just confirm to me my suspicions? Surely, you would try to persuade me that I was delusional, mistaken, or some such thing. That would mean I could accept that and go home. Why are you looking so... distressed?"

"D'yu mind if I smoke?" asked Pat, her hand reaching shakily for her cigarettes.

"No, it's fine, go ahead."

Pat lit one and took a very deep drag. The smoke calmed her, and a soothing feeling spread all over her. These cigarettes were exceptional.

"Okay, I'm ready... I'm ready. I confirmed your suspicions coz I hate lyin' you might as well know that I suspected as much and now I'm bloody 'ere stuck away from me garden and all the girls, me jobs, all what I worked for 'as been scrunched up and thrown away because it was deemed necessary for me to follow you over 'ere followin' your misfortune. I ain't making sense, am I?"

Pat took another long drag.

"I ain't blamin' you, by the way. I reckon I'd have ended up over this side any'ow."

"What do you mean by 'this side?' And what misfortune are you talking about? Michael's death? Is that it?" Pauline's eyes gleamed with tears.

"No it ain't that. It's that you're the first to be selected for a new scientific experiment."

"What? What are you talking about? I've had enough of this! I've been patient with you but you're making no sense! Where is my husband? Why is Bim not here?"

Pat exhaled slowly, fixing her eyes on Lady Nkosi. She spoke calmly. "He's headin' back to London today," Pat looked at her watch. "He left an hour ago."

"He left without me?"

"No... You were with him."

Chapter 28

"I read somewhere that blind people often suffer from depression... especially if they lose their sight later on in life... It's different if you're born blind. You can kind of normalise it... but sudden unexpected blindness in later life..."

Jasmine massaged gently around her now useless eyes, feeling her lashes brush against her thumbs.

"You aren't planning on sleeping then, Jas?" Charlotte murmured groggily from her uncomfortable ball, back-to-back with Bernadine, who was sandwiched between them.

"Sleeping makes a lot of sense as the time'll go quicker till the lights go on."

"Ah, light. Such a simple thing, yet it's the basis for everything we know... everything we are."

"Don't get all fucking philosophical on me, Jas."

"Well, it's a lot better than my ghost stories."

Charlotte groaned and sat up. She was dreadfully chilled and uncomfortable. Her hands were like cold rubbery puppets, and her feet were too.

"If I were on the telly right now, I'd leap up spectacularly and reveal some kind of genius master plan involving saving us all and rescuing Tilly and Pat to boot... with an epic car chase."

"I wouldn't bother rescuing Pascal, though..." Jasmine added,

"And there aren't any cars around here."

"Don't be cruel," said Bernadine, her voice shaking slightly from the cold.

"I'd have us mounted on beautiful horses riding up the beach with the sun pouring onto our backs." Charlotte continued, ignoring both Bernadine and Jasmine.

"Or maybe an outdoor pool and iced drinks served on silver trays."

"Don't talk about ice. I know I've turned blue already, I've lost all sense in my feet. I'm bloody freezing." CRACK!

A loud mechanical humming surrounded them and all at once, the court lit up with blinding white clarity. All three women cried out as their eyes seared with pain and water ran uncontrollably down their cheeks. They crouched defensively, covering their faces, only affording tiny glimmers of razor-sharp light between their fingers, teasing their huge pupils to shrink.

"Charlotte, Charlotte!" Jasmine gasped. There was no response.

A loud thump told of the door crashing open and two figures entered the court. The unmistakable large frame of Mr Wilks and a tall woman dressed in a gown with head and face covering. She seemed distressed and took the arm of the man as if to restrain him. He shook her off with contempt and, with a terrifying mix of elation and aggression, marched towards two of the women who cowered in the centre of the room, their eyes still painful and streaming.

"Where is Charlotte?" he demanded, scouring the room.

"I don't know." Trembled Bernadine.

Drawing herself up to her full height, Jasmine, though her eyes were still raw, looked evenly at the angry man.

"Even if I did know where she was, I would never tell you."

"Jasmine, no!" Pleaded Bernadine.

The head-scarved woman came up behind the group.

"Mr Wilks, control yourself. Remember your Bible, remember the good Lord's words."

The voice was instantly recognisable to both Jasmine and Bernadine, who looked with surprise at Mother Pascal, who was hidden behind the headscarf.

"Mother Pascal?" Bernadine wept.

"Be strong, my child."

284

"To hell with your preaching, woman!!" roared Mr Wilks as he stepped over the crouching Bernadine and grabbed the throat of Jasmine, who began choking and gagging at his grip.

"You've been taught well, haven't you?" He sneered.

"Hiding behind the courage of your absent friend. Where is she now, huh?"

He brought his face close to hers,

"I'll ask you again. Where is Charlotte?"

Finally pushing Jasmine away by her throat, he watched as she struggled to recover, choking and coughing, her streaming eyes darted about the room. She, too, could not think where her friend had gone.

"Search the room! Why did you leave the door open? Useless bloody woman! Go and search!"

Pascal became visibly distressed, her face betraying some awful premonition. Stammering to speak, she finally said,

"I... I will not leave this room until you accompany me back. You must... you must control yourself."

Wilks, surging with anger, spun away from Pascal and turned his eyes to Jasmine, who, though stooped, was recovering quickly.

Hatred burned in her eyes.

"You do not realise... half-cast thing... that you are not protected. There is a debt on your head. You didn't know that, did you?" He smiled wickedly, enjoying the confusion on the young woman's face.

"Let me elaborate... You have not been paid for. Your benefactor died. Last month."

"You... are nothing... but a coward," Jasmine managed to whisper, her spirit dropping as his terrible words sunk in.

She had heard of previous red shirts having a debt on their head. They always disappeared. No one knew where.

"Who put you here? Do you even know? Was it the white Mama of yours ashamed of having a black baby?" His mouth twitched with mockery.

Jasmine pulled herself up, both hands at her throat, but the face held a quiet dignity. She stared levelly ahead.

"Your life counts for nothing here if there is no payment. Perhaps you could have remained with a slave-like status, saved by your own... your own hard work... or something... like that," he snarled, tiny flecks of spittle glinting on his chin.

"But I have the power to decide... your fate... I can keep you alive or strike you down dead right here, right now."

Jasmine continued to stare unblinking, her chin raised slightly so that she looked down upon the enraged man. The corners of her lips lifted by small increments, allowing her to take pity on him.

"Still, you look at me like that!" He threw his fist across her face, a sickening crack echoed about the room. She fell like a rag doll and her skull bounced off the floor, eyes open but not seeing.

Bernadine crumpled where she stood, Pascal threw herself at Wilks but was easily thrown aside.

Jasmine fell with grace, like a wounded soldier. The stamping boots that crushed the life out of her were but war drums on the horizon, distant and inconsequential. Her face held a coolness, a dignity, as her body broke over and over.

The murderer heaved great breaths, eyes alight with gruesome fascination at what he had done, what he had achieved. He turned away and vomited.

Chapter 29

"I wish to make a complaint." Mother Pascal stood in front of a panel.

"Please take a seat, Pascal."

"Thank you."

"You sounded the distress alarm on your device, so this meeting is to log your complaint and to close the case promptly. We need to ascertain why you felt it necessary to sound the code red alarm. Is that understood?"

"Yes."

"So, explain," the moustached man prompted.

"I witnessed a murder... a cold blooded, evil... murder of an innocent..."

"I would be grateful if you were to refrain from such emotive language. Please stick to facts only."

Heather Pascal closed her eyes for a moment and took a short breath as if to compose herself.

"Mr Wilks trampled Jasmine to death in plain sight of both myself and Bernadine. Her murder was carried out with incomprehensible cruelty..."

"Thank you." A suited man beside the man with the moustache took a note and then nodded.

The panel conferred quietly, using their devices to share documents and photographs as evidence. From the body language, Pascal could see that there was some initial conflict. However, it seemed to get resolved quickly. The man with the moustache appeared to chair the proceedings, and his voice spoke conclusively to Pascal.

"The unfortunate girl was a known troublemaker and, as I understand it... on borrowed time. I appreciate that it cannot have been... pleasant... to witness her... her end, however, you of all people, should know that the Abbey works most effectively when the staff are left to carry out their duties undisturbed. You have duties to fulfil, as does Mr Wilks. We are all cogs Pascal. You would do well to remember that. Faulty Cogs are removed swiftly so as not to corrupt the workings of the machine."

"But..."

"Mr Wilks was acting on orders. These orders are not your concern. I accept that you found witnessing his duty morally difficult, it might, therefore, be useful for you to know that Jasmine was unfortunately working against this institution from the very outset and even escaped from Mr Stramford's memorial service for a considerable amount of time in order to infiltrate the sensitive workings of the Abbey."

"I really doubt that Jasmine could..."

"She hid her tablet device with Charlotte's as she entered the service, then ran across the grounds to the concealed entrance of the Research Centre. She was caught spying. She was seen by our Chief of Security. This is no innocent woman, Pascal, much as you would like it to be so."

"But I..."

"She was seen, Pascal. There is nothing you can say to defend her... Unless you have sympathies for her cause?" The man's voice quietened dangerously.

"No, no! Of course not. I... I am as appalled as you are, sir... I had no idea that she was carrying out such... treachery. I had thought she was hard working and of good character, thus my shock at her... brutal... murder."

"It was the removal of disease within the system. Your term 'murder' is not recognised here. Murder is the slaying of another for no reason but wickedness. What you witnessed was a planned assassination," the man stood, chair legs scraping behind him.

"You have wasted my time by calling a code red, and I strongly advise you to think very hard about pressing that button again. It is for emergencies only. You are not to speak of this incident again."

"I... I... yes. Yes, sir," Pascal steadied her shaking hands.

"That is all."

The sink was full. Pans half filled with soapy water that had gone cold. Dirty plates had hardened, leaving tides of residue. Lip marks about the glasses. Paper napkins scrunched in greasy balls.

"In the name of God! What is going on here? Mama mia! This is ridiculous!"

Romano threw his hands up in disbelief.

"Where are my staff, huh? Where are they?"

Wiping his head on his apron, he pulled it off, throwing it to the wash pile, then stomped out of the kitchen.

A silent figure entered and ran quickly down to the storeroom. Crates of peppers, bags of onions and piles and piles of rice and potatoes. Charlotte pulled away at the boxes and packages, revealing a dark and snug hidey-hole. Burrowing inside, she blocked herself in with a bag of onions. The flour bag she lay upon was actually quite comfortable and within minutes, the exhausted woman fell into a deep sleep.

Chapter 30

Patricia stood between the two beds, staring at both occupants as they lay in a deep sleep. She had paced the room numerous times. Checked the IV drips, administered nutrient packs on the hour, and ensured all equipment was working correctly and effectively, but she just could not settle. Her heart was somersaulting around her chest, adrenaline surging around her body.

Where had she come from and what had she become? Taking a step forward, she looked again. The girl on the left bed was mangled and burnt, hair all but gone aside from tufts that grew oddly. The mouth was ajar, exposing drying teeth and grinning like the Cheshire cat.

Hideous. Repulsive.

Her eyes followed the face down from the chin, which had all but melted away down to the neck, showing a rubbery yellow lump of skin and thinner red skin where, beside the thin silver chain of a necklace, Pat could see the gentle pulse working below the surface. Both arms uncovered, one perfect, but the other a ruined stump.

To her right, a Disney beauty with straw-blonde hair that was thick and shiny, and her skin was porcelain with film star proportions. Her closed eyes revealed thick dark eyelashes, a neat little nose, and rosebud lips, plump with youth. The girl on the right was beautiful.

Pat took deep breaths, looking from one to the other. This was hard.

The door opened and a Pascal clone entered.

"You will need to ensure that any jewellery, any personal artefacts are transferred. Her parents are coming in an hour."

The door shut.

Miserably, Pat moved over to burnt Tilly and gently unclasped the St Christopher necklace. It was not dissimilar to her own. The pretty silver thing glinted as it swung on its chain. Carefully, Pat fastened the still warm necklace around Tilly's doppelganger's throat.

A large saloon car swept up the driveway. Within the Bentley were two parents, arriving to collect their daughter. They owed a huge debt to The Abbey for their tireless and groundbreaking work healing their child. Upon meeting her again, they would hand over payment of staggering proportions, signing legal papers to ensure no word of her recovery could ever be traced. A Disney story with a fairytale ending.

Meanwhile, burnt Tilly began to rouse herself. Confused at her whereabouts, she called out for help. Pat rushed in and, without knowing why, embraced the burnt girl as her own.

Tilly, surprised and yet moved, pulled Pat away from her to study her face.

"Pat? Pat, what's wrong? Why are you upset? You can see I'm okay. At least, I think I am. Am I!?"

"Yes, love, yer alright. Yer safe 'ere."

"What the hell is going on? I was playing bloody badminton five minutes ago, then I was taken away... then God knows?! Is this a dream?"

"No love, this ain't no dream."

From within her hiding place, Charlotte could hear very clearly, though she could not see a thing. She felt better from the sleep. However, it did not take long till her mind replayed the terrible scene of Jasmine's death, sickeningly crushed under the heavy boots of the man who now pursued her.

"I try again, again, I am always trying to send out the best food for all the tastes, from the canteen to the most special of the guests, Old Romano. I always rely on Old Romano, but where is Romano's staff, huh? How can I cut if my knives are not washed?!"

Romano's voice increased and decreased in volume as he marched about the kitchen, often nipping down to the storeroom to fetch something or another. Charlotte heard the unmistakable sound of him uncorking a bottle and swigging the contents on a number of occasions before hiding it back amongst the other bottles with a clink.

"Yes, you! Who sent you? Yes, okay, okay, off you go to the washing up, you got a lotta to do. You haven't got a friend, no? Well, get busy. I give you juice or something if you finish within the hour, huh?"

Eventually, Charlotte could bear her self-built prison no longer and, after a good half hour of silence, started to wriggle free. Suddenly, she stopped dead. She revealed a small window with her movements, and there stood a figure. It was large and swaying slightly, its back to her. Without reason, it fell heavily to the floor and remained there, seated. The swaying took up again, and once Charlotte's initial shock of the discovery washed through, she managed to stay completely still.

Mr Romano's voice could suddenly be heard again from up in the kitchen,

"Ah okay! You are doing okay. This is not bad at all. You don't put the cutlery on the same tray, though, Freddie! The cutlery has its own tray. Do you see the mesh one? Yeah! So they don't fall through, yes? Okay, so have some orange juice before you go. Good job, Freddie, good job!"

Footsteps told of Freddie leaving and Mr Romano heading down to the storeroom to fetch his own drink. But he stopped.

"What the? Who is zis in my storeroom?"

He came cautiously down the last few steps to discover Mr Wilks slumped against the bags of flour, head between his hands.

"Wilks? What the name of Mary are you doing in my storeroom, huh? What has happened to you man, you looka terrible. Like a ghost or... something."

"Get me a drink."

"What drink are you saying, Wilks? A juice? A cordial, something fizzy, no?"

"A fucking drink, man!" he growled.

"Okay, okay, I understand, you English, you like a drink, I understand."

Reaching into his secret stash, Mr Romano pulled out a bottle of Port and handed it to Wilks while he wandered about under the guise of looking for a glass. Mr Wilks swigged noisily straight from the bottle.

"I need more. More of whatever you've got. I'm going to hell. I may as well go drunk."

"Hey Hey! Don't talk of hell, sir! What have you been doing? You can talk to Old Romano. Just confess whatever you have done and you can seek forgiveness from the good Lord himself. Rest his soul."

Romano fished about in his pockets for his rosary beads.

"Here, take these. If I am in a bad time... This is what I am doing to help... you need to remember your prayers, Wilks."

"Fuck your prayers", growled Wilks emptying the bottle.

"Nothing is going to save my dirty soul."

"Ah, now, do not disrespect our Lord and Saviour. It is when you are at your lowest, He is by your side... come, come. All is not lost."

Charlotte looked hard through her voyeur's window and was surprised to see a single tear shining its way down Wilk's bristled face. The whole face was that of the most acute despair, so much that Charlotte was shocked to feel a strange compassion for him building about her.

"'Ave a drunk soldier, it is not an easy life 'ere. I don't know much about your duties, but I know we all suffer. 'Ave a nip of sherry with me. I keep it only for my own personal use, for Christmas, you understand, huh? But I think you need it now, Wilks? Am I right or no?"

Charlotte watched in amazement as the face of Mr Wilks contorted into that of deepest misery, tears flowed freely down his cheeks and an eerie wail came from within. His whole body shuddered as Mr Romano passed him a neat little glass of sherry.

"I'm done for Romano. I'm not fit for anything. Just kill me now." Wilks' voice ruptured as he cried freely.

Moving away from the broken figure in his storeroom, Mr Romano studied him with a thoughtful finger on his chin. Muttering to himself in Italian, he walked small circles about the room, finally stopping to look compassionately at the man.

"Okay, Wilks, this is what I am to do..."

Wilks raised his head to look up at the inflated Italian chef, arms resting on his belly.

"You 'ave to sleep this off, whatever troubles you needs a sleeping, so I leave my storeroom open, sir. I leave it as long as you need it. When I come back in the morning for breakfast, you are to be gone and we never talk of this again, comprende?"

The miserable man nodded. The rosary beads swayed from his fingers.

"You keep those till you make peace with God huh? You return them when you have, Wilks. Yes?"

"Yeah."

Mr Romano took one last swig of something, his eyes not leaving Mr Wilks, then replaced the bottle and turned to go. As he did so, he looked directly at Charlotte.

Chapter 31

Pat returned to her room. It was late. The day had felt long and difficult. Though the room was well-ventilated, Pat missed the fresh air that swept in from the small cabin window she used to share with Charlotte. She wondered what she was up to, where she was.

Her new room was sparse, just a bed and a small table with a large bound Bible. A simple chest of drawers containing identical clothes and a small kettle and fridge in the corner. All that she owned was her St Christopher necklace. Sitting on the edge of her bed, she tenderly picked up the coin and studied the small Saint.

"I don't know what I am no more," she told it.

The Saint said nothing, but at least he felt warm.

As Pat began to undress and get ready for bed, she noticed hasty footsteps pacing about the corridor. Re-buttoning her shirt, she moved to the door and popped her head out to see a very distressed Mother Pascal hastily whispering to Pat's clone two doors up. She pointed to Pat and Pascal immediately turned and made haste down the corridor.

"I must come in, I need a word."

Pat motioned for her to sit on the bed, noting her dishevelled appearance. Her headscarf had fallen to her shoulders and her hair looked strangely wild.

"I need to tell someone what has happened, and I have been ordered to stay silent, but I cannot anymore."

Pascal's voice wavered.

"I cannot."

"It's alright, you're 'ere now, there ain't no one gonna bother us." She put her hand upon the distressed lady's arm, but she pulled it away.

"Jasmine has been murdered, crushed to death in front of my eyes. I still hear her bones breaking now. It is too, too horrible."

Her voice came in sharp whispers.

"Murdered? By whom? How?"

Pascal sat bolt upright on the bed, her legs crossing, then uncrossing again.

"This is very hard, Patricia. I'm afraid everything I ever understood about the Abbey has been a betrayal. Jasmine was crushed to death under the boots of... of Mr Wilks. I am sickened... sickened to the stomach."

"Okay." She paused.

"Okay. Hang on m'love. I'm gonna get you some tea. I know ye don't smoke, but I'm gonna insist this time."

She moved to the small kettle in the corner of her room and began to fill it, all the while watching Heather Pascal from the corner of her eye. She remained bolt upright, staring at the wall.

"You take sugar, love?"

"Just black" she murmured.

"No milk? Have a splash."

Pat pulled over her small side table with two steaming cups of tea and a small white plate with Custard Creams. "It ain't very fancy, but it'll do, right?"

Pascal accepted her tea, her expression softening.

"I'm very grateful... I realise I have been rather sharp with you in the past. For that, I am sorry."

"Oh hell, forget it! 'ave a biscuit' Pat nodded reassuringly. "It's no matter, we're 'ere now."

There was a silence as Pat waited for Pascal to talk, but she did not.

"It might sound mad but are ye absolutely sure Jasmine is actually dead? The reason I'm askin' is, you know how all the science and research stuff that goes on 'ere. Wilks didn't just stage that attack to upset yu, did he? He 'as an 'orribly unhealthy lust for power that man."

"No, Patricia. What I saw was like a... a... bestial... brutal... depraved... I heard her bones crack... her ribs snapped like twigs... I saw blood welling in the corners of her mouth. I will never unsee what I saw... It was as if I were witnessing the crucifixion of our Lord Jesus Christ."

Pascal choked and pulled out a tissue from her pocket. Dabbing at each eye, she continued.

"Worse Patricia, I pressed the panic alarm... but instead of retribution... Wilks was pardoned, and I was given a warning for misconduct. I stood in the boardroom... and like a coward... like a coward, I..."

Pascal stopped, struggling to compose herself.

"I condoned their decision. Like Peter betraying Jesus... I said Jasmine's behaviour was appalling..."

"It's called survival, Heather."

Pat took out a cigarette, took a long drag, and then handed it to Pascal.

Pascal put the cigarette between her lips and sucked the smoke deep into her lungs. It swirled around, making her head spin and for a moment, her face relaxed.

"They ain't normal cigarettes, Pascal. I think Stramford created them in his lab for himself but also to make sure I could smoke 'em long after he was gone, I guess, as a sorta thank you? But I dunno."

Pascal turned to Patricia and smiled weakly, exhaling the smoke slowly, she allowed her posture to droop just slightly.

"They are rather good." She inhaled again.

"I know Stramford was fond of you. He rescued you from a life of depravity, didn't he?"

"Yeah, well, I ain't no flower, but enough about that."

She paused, puffed on the cigarette and continued,

"Jasmine was a gem, as bold as Charlotte, as beautiful as they come. Why would Wilks kill 'er? So brutal, too. I've never seen anythin' like that all the time I've been 'ere... Which is a long time."

Both women paused, taking small sips of tea.

"Charlotte escaped, you know," said Pascal after a pause.

"I do not know how, though I suspect she must have been behind the door. I left the door open behind me when we entered."

"Did she see what Wilks did to Jasmine?"

"I think so... although I can't know for certain. We all have to be careful, Patricia. It would seem that we are all disposable."

"Some more than others, right? That's what it was, wasn't it? Jasmine 'ad a debt on 'er head, didn't she? Fuck's sake."

Pascal nodded sadly.

"I knew assassinations took place and of course, I knew we administered euthanasia to many of our clients over time, but it was always done with such dignity. It was for the greater good. It all made complete sense."

"Until it fuckin' didn't."

"Until it didn't."

"If Wilks has had 'is orders from the top, it took away all responsibility from 'im. What I'm wonderin' over and over is how they could've convinced a Christian man... or indeed any man to commit murder. Was the capability there within 'im the whole time? Or was he threatened or... or brutalised to do it?"

Pascal stared vacantly ahead and after some time, very quietly, she whispered,

"I never thought of it like that. I had just assumed he was acting on his own... urges... you think he was somehow forced to do that?"

"I just dunno. I know Wilks can be an asshole, but murder is just a whole differen' level... I can't get me 'ead round it."

There was a long pause as the two women digested their thoughts.

"I used to believe that this place, conceptualised from the love of our Father in Heaven, bore all the signs of civilisation and progression, where suffering was eradicated, where ills were cured... and for a long time, it was! It did!"

Pascal's hands shook slightly as she clasped her tea.

"Now look, the Abbey has become too powerful. They have forgotten the words of Jesus Christ. And now... such an evil ethos puts the Abbey's worth above Christian doctrine. Unless we can contribute something beneficial to this place... we are executed... we are no longer useful... like soldiers sent to war."

The two women became subdued. The dregs of tea were stone cold.

"What 'ave we come to?" Whispered Pat.

Charlotte's breath came out in clouds, though she was not cold. Romano's thick overcoat enveloped her small frame, cosy and protective. Wilks still lay in a drunken slumber sprawled across the storeroom floor. As Charlotte stepped noiselessly over him, she considered possible actions she could take. Smothering him to death with a huge bag of flour? She couldn't lift it. Throwing overripe tomatoes at his drunken, murderous face? His mouth gaped open with every snore. How could she avenge Jasmine's terrible death? The kitchen would be full of knives, she could just stab him through the heart or slice his throat like a gammon steak... The idea, though appealing, repulsed her and with a shudder, she took one final glance and stole up the steps into the kitchen. Romano's great jacket lay on a chair with packets of biscuits and fruits in a pile as if for a picnic. A bottle of fruit juice, cheese, chocolate. Charlotte smiled. So he really had seen her cowering in his storeroom. Her face soon altered as her packed lunch revealed the conspiratorial glint of a sharp kitchen knife, partially concealed under the grapes.

Refreshed and fed, Charlotte pulled on the coat and whatever rations she could fit in the large pockets, along with the kitchen knife. Noting the time on the kitchen clock, she made her way to the heavy outside door. She was going to have to tread familiar ground as an alien, a felon. But what had she done? She had escaped near certain death and now was condemned to hide in the shadows.

Chapter 32

Along the winding country lane crept two black Mercedes in convoy. The cars contained a diplomat and his family. Fractionally ahead of schedule, the driver of the first vehicle slowed to a crawl.

James, head of security, received a notification on his tablet that the visitors were approaching earlier than expected and would be arriving at the Abbey gates within the next ten minutes. With exasperation, he chucked his freshly poured coffee into the sink, grabbed his overcoat, gun, and security radio and covered the lot with his formal overcoat. Knocking his hat off the peg and onto his head, he exited his flat. The ground vibrated as the large grass tile slid open, allowing James to run up the stairs and head toward the line of oaks. He broke into a run as he could already see a small welcoming party gathering by the Abbey's main entrance. It was getting dark, though the Abbey was lit up impressively.

Reaching the entrance gates, James saw with relief that there were no cars there yet. After taking a few good breaths to steady himself, he straightened up.

Standing to attention at the gates, it was not long before James became aware of another person close by. He could hear breathing and, once, just audible throat clearing. Surprised, James slid his hand into his coat and placed it on his gun holster. This was not good timing.

"Show yourself," he ordered.

A rustling came from behind one of the trees.

"I repeat, show yourself. I am armed."

James took his gun out of its holster and pointed it at the rustling tree. After a few moments, a dark-haired, unshaven face came into view, followed by the rest of the man, hands up sheepishly.

"Wilks?!" James put his gun away immediately.

"What the hell are you doing here? Have you been ordered here, too? Surely not looking like that, man! You look... well, you look, off duty, sir!"

"I apologise. I had come only for some fresh air, you know, a walk to clear my head a little."

"Indeed! I can see. Where did you find anything worth drinking in this place?" James asked with amusement.

"Anyhow, I think it best if you scarper, old man. It would not do to be seen here in your current condition."

"Of course, of course, apologies for the... for the shock, old fellow. I'll be on my way."

Tipping his non-existent hat, Wilks slightly staggered back, following the cobbles towards the Abbey.

James watched him go, his gait unsteady as he disappeared into the shadows. Soon, lights appeared behind the gates, winking as the car dipped and peaked on the slightly uneven road surface. With a final notification on his device, James moved to the controls, typed in the code, and placed his thumb on the reader. The huge mechanical gates began to open.

The two sleek cars purred into the grounds. James performed a military salute as the saloons passed him, and then he placed his thumb back upon the reader to close the great gates.

With a jolt, they clanged shut and large bolts mechanically slid across. James turned to follow the cars but froze as a sharp blade pressed warningly against his throat.

"Put your hands in front of you and clasp them together," hissed a hot mouth in his ear.

"One wrong move and this knife slices your neck. Understood?"

James grunted, adrenaline coursing through him. He could hear the cars rumbling over the cobbles as they headed towards the Abbey.

"I am going to take your gun. Keep your hands directly in front of you. Keep them clasped together."

The knife cut into the skin and James felt a sharp sting. A small feminine hand stole under the lapel of his jacket and reached the gun. With some difficulty, the hand released the catch and finally took the pistol from its holster. James continued to feel the knife increase and decrease in pressure as his assailant struggled.

Finally, with a hard shove, James was pushed away, his neck freed from the blade. He stumbled but did not fall. Turning with amazement, he saw his attacker and recognised her at once.

"Well, haven't you become bold?" He said without humour.

"Shut up..." She barked,

"and get onto your knees."

James obeyed, noting how the young woman's hands shook. He did not feel the least bit afraid as he could plainly see that she had no clue how to operate the gun she now pointed at his stomach. Did she even know how to turn off the safety catch?

"What do you want?" He spoke quietly.

"Shut up. I am to ask questions, not you."

There was a pause and the Abbey bells chimed the half hour.

"I can't let you escape, you know. If that is your intention."

"You are not in any position to assert anything at all."

Charlotte glowered at him, emboldened with the gun.

"Open the gate."

"I'm afraid I cannot do that."

"Yes, you can, you just bloody did!"

"Indeed, but that was under orders. I'm afraid I cannot take orders from you."

"Oh, but you can if you have a gun to your head."

Charlotte sharpened her voice.

"I am consigned to carry out my duties, regardless of personal risk to life; therefore, you will have to shoot me first."

"I don't know what the hell you're talking about, but I've had enough. Stand up, put your hands on your head and walk over to the gate."

James stood up obligingly and carried out her request.

"Now open the gate," she demanded, standing a few metres back and pointing the gun insistently.

"No"

"Open the gate, or I'll blow out your brains!"

"No!" Charlotte let out a shout of frustration.

"Are you completely fucking stupid?

"That police-issued gun has not been fitted with a silencer. It is loud," he replied evenly.

"So what?"

"The first shot you fire will alert the Abbey staff. You would do well not to miss it. If you hope to escape, you'll have to be quick. They will scour the grounds until you are found. You will be assassinated on the spot."

"Why are you telling me this?"

"I'm not a monster," he said levelly.

"I'm going to ask you one more time. Open... the... gate."

"You will have to shoot me."

"Then... then you leave me no choice." Charlotte stepped forward, raising the gun.

Her hands shook as she stood no more than two metres from her target.

"I will shoot your kneecaps... that will hurt very, very much, and then you will be forced to open the gate.

"Not if I can't stand."

"Fine! I'll shoot your shoulder... does it really have to come to this?" James shrugged, his hands still on his head.

Suddenly, things happened very fast. Charlotte pointed the gun at James' shoulder and pressed the trigger. There was a click, but the gun did not shoot. James, in one swift movement, knocked the pistol from Charlotte's hand, retrieved the knife from the other and held her in an impossibly tight lock hold.

She began to roar with fear and fury. James ripped off the hood from her coat and swiftly applied it as a gag. Using the knife on the sleeves of the same jacket, he bound her hands together.

"I think you have said enough," pushing Charlotte onto her knees, "This is the second time that you have ruined my evening."

He drew out his tablet from his pocket and scrolled through several notifications. His face clouded.

"This isn't good," he murmured, obviously distressed.

Charlotte moaned behind her gag.

"No, I'm sorry, I'm not releasing you this time. You've caused enough... I need to... I need to think."

He hauled Charlotte to her feet.

"Move" he gestured towards the Abbey.

The two walked in silence along the cobbles, James seemingly struggling with his conscience as he repeatedly looked at his prisoner, bound and gagged. She looked small and vulnerable, wrapped in Mr Romano's oversized coat, wrappers from cheese and hotel biscuits were half trailing from one of her pockets. He could see his makeshift gag was beginning to slip off, though she made no effort to speak.

By the last oak tree, things happened so fast that Charlotte knocked to the ground and hit her head on the cobbles, so she could not ascertain what was going on.

A strong hand grabbed at a throat, a choking and coughing ensued. A thick punch to the stomach doubled over, retching and gasping. Fists clashed and a soft mouth split against teeth.

"Back down, man! Back down!"

A voice gargled,

"Don't resist! I have to follow orders. Comply! Comply, for Christ's sake!"

A gun slid across the cobbles, stopping at Charlotte, who was trying desperately to twist her face out of the mud. Her arms were bound so tightly that she was uselessly immobile. Even her visibility was restricted as her gag dislodged and travelled up and over one eye.

A figure burst out of the fray and ran towards her. Using all her strength, she kicked the gun away. It cartwheeled across the cobbles clinking metallically until finally it rested in a clump of grass. The approaching figure morphed into the wretched Mr Wilks. His eyes wide, a deep purple gash across his cheek and black hair matted against his forehead.

"Charlotte," he gasped, stretching out to touch her.

Recoiling, Charlotte struggled away from him, writhing uselessly on the cobbles. When she finally stopped, she saw he had moved away.

"Don't move, James," Wilks spoke, holding the gun Charlotte had kicked moments before. The gun was pointed directly at James' head. The Chief of Security was in a bad way. He had a nasty mouth injury, and blood ran freely down his chin and onto his chest. His hands were raised in surrender.

"That's Compton's daughter, Wilks. You know that, right?"

"An order is an order, James."

"But why don't you take her to the Abbey jail? Let her face trial?"

"Oh, come on, man! This place has gone to hell. Do you honestly think she'd have a fair trial? She's as good as dead already." He spat on the cobbles, leaving a crimson star.

"You're drunk. You're not in your right mind," James asserted sharply, hands wavering as a combination of fatigue and shock hit him.

"Keep your hands up!" Wilks barked as he moved towards Charlotte again, the gun still pointed at James.

Pulling out Romano's kitchen knife, he crouched by Charlotte, moving his face close to hers. She could smell blood and sweat as his face touched hers. Turning into her hair, he took a series of long, deep breaths as if taking some sustenance from her scent.

She froze, eyes following the knife, which turned from silver to black as it caught, and then threw the light.

"You sweet thing." He inhaled again, shuddering as he exhaled. Utterly repulsed, she felt the wetness of his blood on her ear. With a shout, she twisted out of his grip but saw a flash of the blade. Something ripped behind her and she realised he had sliced through the binding on her wrists. She was free.

She pulled her weary arms forward and threw off the gag that hung loose about her neck. Within moments, her elation dissipated. Her newly liberated hands were forced to pull at the strong arm that now held her by the neck.

"Come," Wilks growled, forcibly moving her over towards James. He pushed her forward and stumbled on his feet.

Picking her up and holding her fiercely, he pointed the gun at James.

"What the hell are you doing?" James raised an eyebrow.

"Carry out your orders if you must, but why are you pointing that thing at me?"

Wilks, deeply troubled, leaned hard on Charlotte, who could feel her legs buckling under his weight. He seemed to be experiencing a wave of some terrible emotion which brought tears down his face. They glistened into the congealed blood on his cheek and for a third time, he twisted his face into Charlotte's hair. The weight of him brought them both down heavily, but even though James jumped up, Wilks still managed to point the gun at his head.

"You will do one thing for me, James. One thing that may lighten my damned fate."

Although James' face bore the wounds of Wilk's fury, there was still compassion etched across it.

"What is it, Wilks? Explain yourself."

With some difficulty, he hauled himself up and kicked Charlotte.

"Get up!"

She looked fearfully at James, who was losing blood fast. There was nothing he could do. He was unarmed and horribly injured.

Finding her voice, she blurted,

"Please just do your orders. Just do it! Leave him alone. He's done nothing to either of us. I can't stand by and watch this any more."

She paused, pulling tendrils of loose hair away from her face. "You're supposed to kill me, right? Like Jasmine? Those are your orders. Just do it! But please, at least afford me some dignity. I... I..."

"You talk far too much," spat Wilks, roughly pushing her forward.

"Move to the gates, both of you."

At the gates, Wilks stared at both of his victims, one bleeding profusely, the other white with fear.

"Open the gate, James" he murmured. There was no response.

"Open the fucking gate!"

"I cannot do that, sir." The security chief spoke resolutely though his eyes betrayed fear.

"You will open the gate alive and willing, or I will haul your dead body up to the reader and use your print to open it myself. I am going to hell either way, James. It's best if I don't take you with me."

With great reluctance, James, with the gun to his head, typed in the code, then pressed his thumb upon the reader. The great gates began to slowly open.

"You coward! You may commit evil... murders, but you won't get far!" Charlotte screamed in a fury.

"Go on and run for freedom like the depraved creature you are!"

Both she and James watched him raise the gun towards them. Moving away from James, he turned his attention to Charlotte. Taking her in his arms, he nestled the gun about her temple. With a strange tenderness, he drew her into a bizarre waltz away from the security pad and towards the open exit. She closed her eyes, waiting for the end, but with an almighty push, Wilks unexpectedly threw her across the threshold, out into the countryside road, out to freedom.

"You're free, run away! Escape from this damned place!"

He shouted after her.

Scrabbling up from the ground, she broke into a run. Her legs buckled as she went, but each time, she hauled herself up, splashing through puddles and gasping for breath. The gates clanged shut behind her. Onwards, she ran, the loose stones scattering noisily as if applauding.

It was only after about a minute she heard a pistol shot resounding in the air.

James watched Wilks turning around and around at the base of the great oak, his face white but for the single gash down his cheek. The bullet had torn through his stomach, shot from relatively far.

His face crumpled in pain as he gasped,

"God forgive me... God forgive me!"

Graham, a well-respected police officer in James' team, had fired the shot following a distress call from James' tablet device. Wilks was to be charged with grievous bodily harm upon the security chief and the lesser offence of drunk and disorderly conduct on duty. He was to be sentenced at the Abbey if he survived the night. The agony of the stomach wound did not allow him to die instantly, but his suffering caused his legs to kick out repeatedly, turning him around and around the base of the oak tree. Blood mixed with mud, his salty tears and saliva adding cocktail finesse for the thirsty roots of the great trees...

James was taken to the Abbey for questioning. He did not admit any knowledge of Compton's daughter being in the area at the time and said his distress signal had only been because Mr Wilks had forcibly taken his gun and was a danger to himself and others. By the time the authorities realised the gate had been opened a second time that evening, many hours had passed and both James and Charlotte's father silently prayed that she had managed to get far enough away from the dangerous surveillance cars that scoured the area for weeks after. Romano hoped that Charlotte had enough cheese, biscuits and grapes to keep her going until she found food and shelter.

Patricia held her St Christopher tight in her fingers as she smiled widely into her empty room.

"You little shit bag, you done it!! You actually escaped this place and made your way 'ome."

She chuckled into the emptiness.

Releasing the pendant, it fell back snugly upon her wrinkled chest. It heard her heart hammering against it, the pulse of hope and admiration from one so confined and shackled to Stramford's Abbey.